CLIVEDEN

Buckinghamshire

THE NATIONAL TRUST

Cliveden is three miles upstream from Maidenhead, two miles north of Taplow.

Acknowledgements
Chapters 1–4, 7 and 8 of this guide was written by Jonathan Marsden while he was Historic Buildings Representative for the National Trust's Thames & Chilterns region, incorporating the passages on architectural history from Gervase Jackson-Stops's 1978 guide. Chapter 5 is by Christopher Wall, for many years Historic Buildings Representative responsible for Cliveden, and for the major repairs in 1983–4, and author, with Graham Stuart Thomas, of the strategic plan for the grounds. Chapter 6 and the Catalogue of Garden Sculpture are by Antonia Boström. For assistance in the preparation of this guide and its illustrations, the National Trust is indebted to Viscount Astor, David Astor, Lord Crathorne, Wendy Hefford, Lord Strathnaver, John Tham, the Duke of Westminster and James Yorke.

Photographs: Aerofilms p.65; British Architectural Library, RIBA, London p.11 (above and below); Cliveden Hotel Ltd pp.38, 93; Colnaghi's London p.19; A.C. Cooper pp.16, 17, 43; Country Life Picture Library p.26; Courtauld Institute of Art p.20; Forschungsarchiv für römische Plastik, Cologne p.78; Greater London Record Office p.12; Carl Laubin/Foundation for Art, National Trust Photographic Library p.77; Malmesbury Charitable Settlement p.7; National Galleries of Scotland p.27; National Portrait Gallery, London pp.9, 10, 42; National Trust p.14; NT/Paul Barkshire pp.57, 58, 59, 61, 84; National Trust Photographic Library pp.45, 52 (above); NTPL/Oliver Benn p.66; NTPL/John Bethell p.70; NTPL/John Blake p.64; NTPL/Vera Collingwood pp.1, 29, 79, 81; NTPL/Derek Croucher front and back covers, p.60; NTPL/John Hammond pp.13, 30, 31, 40, 41, 87, 88, 91, 92, back cover; NTPL/Angelo Hornak front cover, pp.15, 20, 28, 35, 44, 49, 50, 51, 52 (below), 53, 54; NTPL/Nick Meers pp.67, 69, 71; NTPL/Ian Shaw pp.4, 55, 72, 73, 75, 82; Oxfordshire Photographic Archive p.76; Royal Commission on the Historical Monuments of England/Buckinghamshire County Museum pp.32, 33; Sotheby's p.23; the Duke of Westminster p.34.

Revised 2001

ISBN 0 7078 0245 8

Designed by James Shurmer

Phototypeset in Monotype Bembo series 270
by SPAN Graphics Ltd, Crawley, West Sussex (SG1894)

Print managed by Centurion Press Ltd (BAS)
for the National Trust (Enterprises) Ltd,
36 Queen Anne's Gate, London SW1H 9AS

CONTENTS

INTRODUCTION

Cliveden, or Cliefden as it was often spelt until the nineteenth century, owes its name to the chalk cliffs between Maidenhead and Cookham which overlook the flat river basin of the Thames. They were described by the antiquary John Leland in 1538 as 'cliffy ground hanging over the Tamise with some Busshis growing on it' (*Itinerary* of 1538). The cliffs are bisected by a dean, or small valley, and command views across the dean and down the river. There were none of the usual defensive, administrative or agricultural reasons for building a large house here, and there never have been. This commanding prospect has always been Cliveden's *raison d'être*.

The possibilities of the site for building were not recognised until George Villiers, 2nd Duke of Buckingham, acquired the land in about 1666, and began the levelling of a great platform. This guide to Cliveden and its grounds describes not one but three houses, and far from chronicling the continuous descent of a single family, it must tell something of the lives of six. There can be few sites which have seen such an intensity of building over three centuries, and few indeed whose owners have included the holders of three dukedoms, an earldom, and a viscountcy, all of them men of far above average means. What has been built here involved ten architects, and unbuilt designs were provided by a further three, amounting to an architectural development rarely seen outside royal patronage; but in fact the least active period of this development can be found at a time when Cliveden had a royal tenant, Frederick, Prince of Wales.

(Left) The view south down the Cliveden reach of the Thames, which Garibaldi likened to the mighty river prospects of South America. The views over the surrounding landscape have always been Cliveden's raison d'être

The present house was built in 1849–51 to the designs of Sir Charles Barry, architect of the Palace of Westminster. In its expressly Italianate appearance, Cliveden is unusual among English country houses, and in several other respects it is quite outside that tradition. Its position on the Thames within 25 miles of Westminster and five of Windsor Castle made it convenient as a 'summer palace' or retreat from the city; even in the eighteenth century it was possible to lunch in London and dine at Cliveden. Its land has never extended much further than the 'home grounds' that remain today. (It formerly included a 'home farm' across the river at White Place.) For this reason, and because the property has passed through so many hands, most of Cliveden's history involves very little contact with its immediate locality.

The historical chapters that follow concentrate on the owners, builders and gardeners who contributed most to the present appearance of Cliveden: the 2nd Duke of Buckingham, the 1st Earl of Orkney, the 2nd Duke and Duchess of Sutherland, the 1st Duke of Westminster, and three generations of the Astor family. It was the 2nd Viscount Astor who presented the house and grounds, with the collections of sculpture and some of the historic contents of the house, to the National Trust in 1942. His family continued to live here until the death of the 3rd Viscount in 1966. Since only a proportion of the contents remained, it was decided to find a tenant for the house while retaining public access to the principal rooms. From 1966 until 1984 the house was let by the Trust to Stanford University, California, and since 1985 to Cliveden Hotel Ltd for use as an hotel. Through these tenants it has been possible to fulfil Lord Astor's wishes that Cliveden should further 'Anglo-American cooperation' and be a place where a mixture of people can meet.

CHAPTER ONE

THE 2ND DUKE OF BUCKINGHAM
(1666–96)

The man who built the first Cliveden, George Villiers (1628–87), 2nd Duke of Buckingham, was a politician, diplomat, poet, playwright, amateur chemist, gambler, adulterer and murderer. He was born at Wallingford House in Whitehall, which was at the time the residence of his father, the 1st Duke and the notorious favourite of James I and of his son Charles I. Before he was a year old, his father was assassinated at Portsmouth, and George and his brother and sister were brought up with the children of Charles I. He was aged only fifteen and a student at Cambridge at the onset of the Civil War in August 1642, but immediately joined the King's army at Oxford. The following spring his estates were sequestered by Parliament along with those of his younger brother Francis. They were reinstated in return for an undertaking to remain out of the country, and the brothers spent the next four years in France and Italy. Back in England in 1647, they joined the force being assembled in the King's cause by Lord Holland, but in the course of its defeat at Surbiton Francis Villiers was killed, and by the spring of 1649 Buckingham had been outlawed by Parliament. His property was once again confiscated, and he fled to Holland.

The following year he accompanied the new King, Charles II, to Scotland and in 1651 marched south with the Scottish army to the Battle of Worcester. He was suspected of having escaped with the King after their defeat, but made his own way once more to Holland.

Buckingham returned again to England in 1657. By this time he had become alienated from Charles, partly owing to the influence of Edward Hyde, the future Earl of Clarendon, the exiled King's chief adviser, and was applying himself to the recovery of his property. His confiscated estates had been divided between Cromwell himself and General Lord Fairfax, and soon after his return, Buckingham was married to Fairfax's daughter Mary. The Fairfaxes were established in Yorkshire, where much of Buckingham's own property lay, but the alliance between a man whom Parliament had declared a public enemy, and the daughter of their own former commander-in-chief was greeted with suspicion on both sides. To Clarendon it seemed that Buckingham had made an entirely self-interested deal with the Protector; on the other hand Parliament remained fearful of his intentions and ordered his imprisonment. He remained under arrest in the Tower during 1658, securing his release in February 1659 by a pledge not to support the enemies of the Commonwealth. In fact, his activities in pursuit of the restoration of the King were uninterrupted, and carried on much of the time in collaboration with his father-in-law, who led the delegation to Charles II at The Hague in 1660 which brought about his return. At the Restoration, Buckingham regained his estates and was appointed Lord Lieutenant of the West Riding and a Gentleman of the Bedchamber. In the early 1660s he began a steady campaign to supplant Lord Chancellor Clarendon in the King's favour.

As one biographer has written, Buckingham's character and career '. . . contain a scale of contrasts which is both repulsive and bewildering, judged by the standards of today; the tape-measure of the twentieth century shrivels up as it touches this man.'[1] His early travels on the Continent imparted something of the high culture that had made his father the greatest connoisseur of the age after the King. He employed a band of musicians in London that Pepys reckoned 'the beste in Towne' when they came to play at his own house,[2] and he was a patron of poets, above all of Abraham Cowley, who had been with him at Cambridge, and at whose funeral in 1667 the Duke 'held a tassel of the Pall', according to the biographer John Aubrey. It was with

The Duke of Buckingham; by John Michael Wright, 1669 (private collection)

Cowley, and with John Wilmot, 2nd Earl of Rochester, that Buckingham developed his own literary talents. Buckingham and Rochester, an incredibly licentious figure even by the standards of his day, were also frequent companions in debauchery. The Duke's best work, *The Rehearsal*, was performed in 1671, a farce whose humour was largely at the expense of John Dryden. Ten years later, Dryden's revenge came with his characterisation of the Duke as Zimri in *Absalom and Achitophel*:

A man so various that he seemed to be
Not one but all mankind's epitome:
Stiff in opinions, always in the wrong;
Was everything by starts and nothing long;
But in the course of one revolving moon
Was chymist, fiddler, statesman and buffoon;
Then all for women, painting, rhyming, drinking,
Besides ten thousand freaks that died in thinking.

In 1667 the struggle between Buckingham and the Lord Chancellor (the 'B' and 'C' of the 'Cabal' ministry) came to a head. Clarendon had him arrested for having treasonably employed astrologers to forecast the King's downfall. So improbable a charge was the desperate last resort of an increasingly unpopular minister. By December, Pepys recorded that '. . . the Duke of Buckingham doth rule all now',[3] and that the King was his 'slave'. Clarendon was impeached and fled to France, and Buckingham was made chief minister of state.

Around October 1666 Buckingham took as his mistress one of the great court beauties, Anna Brudenell, Countess of Shrewsbury, and it was probably for her that he bought and began building at Cliveden in the late 1660s.[4] At the end of 1667 the Earl of Shrewsbury learnt of their affair and challenged Buckingham to a duel. Pepys records:

. . . they met yesterday in a close near Barne Elmes [near Putney] and there fought; and my Lord Shrewsbury is run through the body from the right breast through the shoulder, and Sir J. Talbot all along up one of his arms, and Jenkins killed upon the place... [Talbot and Jenkins were the Earl's seconds]... This will make the world think that the King hath good councillors about him, when the Duke of Buckingham, the greatest man about him, is a fellow of no more sobriety than to fight about a whore.[5]

The tradition that Lady Shrewsbury was not only present but held her lover's horse while he inflicted fatal injuries on her husband is probably a myth, but she was certainly capable of such callousness; at another time she personally organised a near fatal attack on Harry Killigrew, a former lover, in which his servant was killed. In May 1668 Pepys describes the Duke as having brought Lady Shrewsbury home to his house:

. . . where his Duchess saying that it was not for her and the other to live together in a house, he answered, 'Why, Madam, I did think so; and therefore have ordered your coach to be ready to carry you to your father's'; which was a devilish speech, but they say true.[6]

Although the birth of a son to the Duke and Countess in 1671, and his dubbing (by the Duke) Earl of Coventry further strained the King's tolerance, the Duke's position as a member of the 'Cabal' ministry remained intact.

There are almost no surviving papers to shed light on the Duke's building works at Cliveden. When he died in 1688, it was without an heir and in some obscurity, and a great body of his papers must have been lost. The original landform can also only be imagined, but it is certain that the creation of the flat forecourt on the north side and the much lower and equally artificial parterre on the south must have entailed a massive earth-moving operation. According to George Vertue,[7] the Duke's architect was William Winde, known as 'Captain Winde' after the interruption of a career in military engineering led him into domestic architecture. Few houses can be attributed to him with certainty, but on the evidence of Hampstead Marshall in Berkshire and Combe Abbey in Warwickshire (both for the Royalist Earl of Craven) he is regarded as one of the most innovative architects of his generation.

It is not clear where the idea of the arcaded terrace originated.[8] In 1670 the Duke was sent to France in connection with the secret Treaty of Dover, and with his known Francophile tastes he may have wished to emulate either François Mansart's Orangery at Versailles or his famous terraces above the Seine at St Germain. As a young man he had also visited many of the courts of Italy, and when John Evelyn came to Cliveden in 1679 he described the new house as standing '. . . somewhat like Frascati as to its front', recalling perhaps the Villa Aldobrandini at Frascati east of Rome. On the other hand an even closer source available to Winde would have been Pietro da Cortona's imagined reconstruction of the Temple of Palestrina (Praeneste), published in J. M. Suarez's *Praenestes Antiquae* in 1655. Here, the lowest terrace in a series leading up the hillside to the temple has marked affinities with that at Cliveden. Later reconstructions of this influential Roman ruin suggested attached columns between the arches at Palestrina, which may explain why

these are shown (though apparently never executed) in the engraving of the garden front of Cliveden in *Vitruvius Britannicus* (1717), illustrated on p.11.

The 1717 engraving also shows the arches as concave niches, and according to one source, the Duke intended to fill them with 'statues bigger than the life'.[9] Since no statues appear in the subsequent eighteenth-century engravings it can be assumed they were never installed, but the niches – as opposed to the present blind arcade – do appear in Luke Sullivan's engraving of 1759.

The house itself is known from no contemporary

COUNTESS OF SHREWSBURY.

Sir Peter Lely's portrait of Anna Brudenell, Countess of Shrewsbury, for whom her lover, the Duke of Buckingham, is thought to have bought Cliveden (National Portrait Gallery). A copy is at Cliveden (see p.89)

The Duke c.1675; by Peter Lely (National Portrait Gallery). A copy is at Cliveden (see p.88)

King's favour. Out of power his income dropped and his debts accumulated.

The Duke's last years were spent in and around Helmsley Castle in the East Riding. Out hunting in April 1687, he fell asleep in wet grass, having been thrown when his exhausted horse collapsed beneath him after a long run. He caught a fever and was brought to the house of his brother-in-law at Kirkbymoorside. Here (not exactly, as Pope had it, 'in the worst inn's worst room') he died a few days later:

On once a flock-bed, but repaired with straw,
With tape-tied curtains never made to draw,
The George and Garter dangling from that bed
Where tawdry yellow strove with dirty red,
Great Villiers lies – alas! how changed from him,
That life of pleasure and that soul of whim!
Gallant and gay in Cliveden's proud alcove,
The bower of wanton Shrewsbury and love;
Or just as gay at Council, in a ring
Of mimicked statesmen and their merry king.
No wit to flatter, left of all his store;
No fool to laugh at, which he valued more.
There, victor of his health, of fortune, friends
And fame, this lord of useless thousands ends.[11]

descriptions or images. Lord Orkney's letters (see p.14) make clear that it had four storeys including a high attic, in which respects it may have resembled Ashdown, another Berkshire house of the Cravens, which Winde may also have designed and which is now also the property of the Trust. Of the interior even less is known, but it may be that the 'Spanish Oak' wainscotting and 'fret-work' (ie moulded plaster) ceilings and walnut staircase seen by John Loveday in 1734 survived from the Duke's house.[10]

The house was apparently still in the course of building in 1677 when Buckingham found himself once more in the Tower. He had been dismissed from office in 1674 after parliamentary opposition both to the Shrewsbury affair and the role he had played in the Treaty of Paris. Though he was soon released, the Duke played no further significant part in politics and from 1682 he seems to have retired to Yorkshire. The great estates of his father and those he had acquired by marriage helped to sustain his gigantic expenditure, but for much of his career his income varied dramatically depending on the

NOTES

1 Hester Chapman, *Great Villiers*, 1949, p.105.

2 *Diary*, 6 January 1668.

3 Ibid., 30 December 1667.

4 Buckingham had many other houses: Owthorpe in Northamptonshire, Burley-on-the-Hill in Rutland, a substantial house in York, and Helmsley Castle and a further dozen smaller houses in Yorkshire.

5 *Diary*, 17 January 1668.

6 Ibid., 16 May 1668.

7 *Notebooks*, iv, p.11.

8 Winde has been shown to have worked somewhat later at Powis Castle on the Welsh border, the only other house in Britain with a comparable series of arcaded terraces.

9 Quoted in J. Heneage Jesse, *Memoirs of the Court of England During the Reign of the Stuarts*, 1901 ed., pp.99–100, from an unnamed source of *c*.1700.

10 Sarah Markham, *John Loveday of Caversham, 1711–1789*, 1984, pp.177–8.

11 Alexander Pope, *Epistle to Lord Bathurst, On the Use of Riches*, 1733.

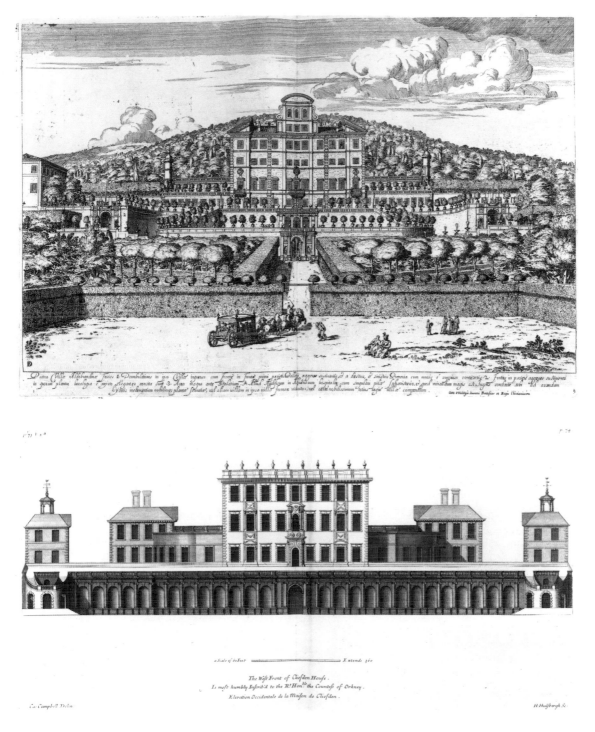

(*Top*) *The Villa Aldobrandini at Frascati; engraving from Domenicus Barrière's 'Villa Aldobrandina Tuscolana' (1647)*
(*Below*) *The garden front of Cliveden, from Colen Campbell's 'Vitruvius Britannicus' (1717)*

CHAPTER TWO
GEORGIAN CLIVEDEN (1696–1824)

Nine years after Buckingham's death, Cliveden was bought by Lord George Hamilton (1666–1737), one of the younger sons of the 1st Earl of Selkirk and of the redoubtable Lady Anne Hamilton, Duchess of Hamilton in her own right. Hamilton was a career soldier, first commissioned at the age of eighteen and appointed lieutenant-colonel in 1689 under William of Orange, whose friend he became. In November 1695 he married one of the King's former mistresses, Elizabeth Villiers, who was also his cousin and a kinswoman of the late Duke of Buckingham.

Early in 1696 Hamilton was created Earl of Orkney, and it was later in that year that he purchased Cliveden, apparently for its proximity to Taplow and Windsor. Despite what his marriage may have brought him, he had to borrow many of the necessary funds, persuaded that it would be cheaper to buy an existing house than build a new one. His finances seem to have remained insecure, since he made little or no alteration to house or estate for ten years.

Lord Orkney was promoted major-general in 1702, and lieutenant-general in 1704. In that year he served as second-in-command to the Duke of Marlborough at Blenheim, where he captured 8,000 enemy soldiers and 800 officers, '... perhaps the greatest and compleatest victory that has been gained this many aiges', as he called it in a letter shortly afterwards.[1] He played a prominent part in the subsequent battles of the War of the Spanish Succession: Ramillies (1706), Oudenarde (1707), and Malplaquet (1709). In the last action he opened the allied attack at the head of fifteen battalions. Despite their success he wrote of the losses on that day '... in many places they lye as thick as ever you saw a flock of sheep ... I hope in God it will be the last battle I may ever see. A very few of such would make both parties end the war very soon.'[2] Something of the character of these hostilities can be seen in the tapestries that survive at Cliveden from the *Art of War* set woven for Orkney.[3]

(Left) George Hamilton, 1st Earl of Orkney (1666–1737); by John Michael Rysbrack

(Right) 'Embuscade', one of the 'Art of War' Brussels tapestries woven for Lord Orkney to commemorate his prominent role in the Marlborough Wars. Three of the series now hang in the Hall

The north front of Lord Orkney's house; engraving by John Donowell, 1752

Although Jonathan Swift recorded that Lady Orkney 'squints like a dragon', he also considered her the wisest woman he ever knew. Francis Godolphin, the Lord High Treasurer, found her 'extreamly medling' in affairs of state, remarking that between her and the Duke of Shrewsbury (the greatest intriguer of his day) 'tis hard to determine which is the greater politician ...'[4] Some years later, Lady Mary Wortley Montagu provided the most memorable description of this unfortunate woman as she took part in the coronation procession of 1727:

She exposed behind a mixture of fat and wrinkles, and before a considerable pair of bubbies a good deal withered, a great belly that preceded her; add to this the inimitable roll of her eyes and her grey hair which by good fortune stood directly upright, and 'tis impossible to imagine a more delightful spectacle.[5]

Among her attractions at the time of their marriage, however, Hamilton may have found the fact that six months earlier the King had granted her almost all the private estates of James II in Ireland.

What is known of Lord Orkney's first improvements at Cliveden is contained in one volume of family letters now in the National Library of Scotland.[6] His letters to his younger brother Lord Archibald Hamilton reveal his continuing anxiety over money and indecision as to design. The great height of Buckingham's house, and of the rooms on the top floor, did not suit him:

... we think of tacking away the Garretts and lowering the next story to the Garets which will take away near twenty foot of the height of the House and building a sort of wings like burley House for offices.

This is in effect what was carried out some time soon afterwards, but not before Orkney had 'had the opinion of sevrall of the chiefe men in England', including Marlborough himself, who 'bid me get my whole desine and doe one part this year [ie 1706] and soe by degrees ...'[7]

Surviving designs for the wings and the colonnades which connected them to the house confirm their attribution in *Vitruvius Britannicus* (1717) to Thomas Archer (*c*.1668–1743),[8] who had recently

View of Cliveden from the south in the mid-eighteenth century; a copy by an unknown artist of the 1759 engraving of Luke Sullivan's drawing. It shows the garden front of the Orkney house and Leoni's Octagon Temple (collection Viscount Astor)

completed a new north front at Chatsworth in Derbyshire and could certainly rank as one of the 'chiefe men' in architecture at the time. Like Winde before him, Archer was strictly an 'amateur' or 'gentleman-architect', but among his contemporaries his designs bore the closest relation to the European Baroque, in churches such as St John's Smith Square at Westminster, or extravagant garden pavilions such as those at Chatsworth and Wrest Park in Bedfordshire. Beside these, his Cliveden buildings seem uninteresting, but an unexecuted plan in the Cliveden Album suggests that a complete rebuilding was at one stage intended.[9] The house as Archer left it is known only from the plates in *Vitruvius Britannicus* and other engravings, since it was destroyed by fire in 1795; the colonnades were pulled down to prevent the spread of the second fire in 1849, and the wings completely remodelled by Barry thereafter (see p.29).

It is perhaps more in the garden and wider landscape (see Chapter Five) that Orkney's work at Cliveden recalls the lines of his acquaintance Alexander Pope: 'Our generals, now retired to their estates, hang up their trophies on their gates'. Designs by the Venetian immigrant Giacomo Leoni (*c*.1686–1746) of around 1727 for the so-called Blenheim Pavilion at the northern end of the garden survive in the Cliveden Album. Orkney is said to have 'figured the battle at Blenheim, by plantations of trees, now in full vigour',[10] but apart from an otherwise unexplained sequence of square blocks of trees shown to the east of the house in eighteenth-century surveys, there is no evidence to support this tradition. Although Pope was advising Lord Orkney in the 1730s, this pavilion, and Leoni's other contribution, the Octagon Temple (1735), which hangs above the Thames to the south-west of the house and enjoys views both up and down the river, seem to belong more to the world of William Kent and the wider 'prospect' than to that of Pope's enclosed alcoves and bowers.

The Cliveden Album contains several more drawings by Leoni, which appear to be designs for the rebuilding of the house. If so, then like Archer's earlier proposal they were certainly never executed. They can be seen as a further indication of the financial frustrations that seem always to have constrained Lord Orkney's gardening and building ambitions, while several of his fellow 'retired' generals, most notably Lord Cobham at Stowe in Buckinghamshire (with whom Orkney had both Bridgeman and Leoni in common[11]), could indulge to the full their appetites for these activities.

After the accession of George I in 1714, Lord Orkney was appointed governor of Virginia (a position he held until his death, without ever visiting America), and Lord of the King's Bedchamber. In July 1717 he was one of the small company on the King's barge for the first performance of Handel's *Water Music*, and the King was entertained at Cliveden in 1724.

Lord Orkney died in 1737 and was buried at Taplow. He was succeeded in his property and titles by a daughter, Anne, who became Countess of Orkney in her own right. In 1720 she had married her first cousin William O'Brian, 4th Earl of Inchiquin in the peerage of Ireland. Their home was Taplow Court, neighbouring Cliveden to the south, and on Lord Orkney's death they let the Cliveden estate to Frederick Louis, Prince of Wales (son of George II and father of George III), who held it until his death in 1751.

'Poor Fred' had a bad press, at a time when the language of the press was particularly hard. Lord Hervey compared the Prince of Wales to Nero, and Horace Walpole never had a good word for him, but they were hardly neutral witnesses, being respectively the *confidant* of his estranged mother

(Left) Frederick, Prince of Wales (1707–51), who leased Cliveden from 1737 until his death; after Jean-Baptiste van Loo (Staircase)

(Right) Frederick, Prince of Wales with his sisters, the Princesses Anne, Caroline and Amelia at Kew; by Philippe Mercier, c.1733 (Hall)

and the son of the Prime Minister against whom he so often found himself aligned.[12] Frederick was born in the palace of Herrenhausen in Hanover in 1707. When the Elector George Augustus ascended the British throne in 1714, he brought his son (the future George II) to England, leaving his young grandson in Hanover. George II also preferred to keep his twenty-year-old heir out of his way in Hanover, and when Frederick did arrive in England in 1728, he became a focus and a putative leader of the political opposition.

In the years before his tenancy of Cliveden the Prince was continually at odds with his father, usually over his allowance, and became at the same time a hero of the popular opposition and the instrument of a group of Whig politicians united in opposition to Sir Robert Walpole. It was in the aftermath of a parliamentary debate on his allowance (and the question of a jointure for the Princess – Augusta of Saxe-Gotha, whom the Prince had married in 1736) that the Prince was formally excluded from Court and established himself at Cliveden. At around the same time he acquired Park Place, further along the Thames near Henley, from the late Lord Orkney's brother Lord Archibald Hamilton.[13]

The Prince evidently used Cliveden rather as Louis XIV had used the château of Marly south of Paris – as a retreat from London where he could enjoy the society of his close friends. However, Joseph Farington noted in his diary that 'he carried state very high in some respects, never admitting any persons of whatever rank to dine with Him and the Princess at Cliefdon House ...'[14] Most of the Prince's life at Cliveden seems to have been taken up with racing, cards, music, cricket and drinking (sometimes in the predecessor of the Feathers Inn by the main gate, named at this time, in the Prince's honour, the Three Feathers). Although the old Duchess of Marlborough wrote to Lord Stair in 1738 that among his other mounting debts there was '... a good deal of expense at Cliveden in building and furniture',[15] nothing that survives there can be attributed to him with certainty. At some stage between 1717, when elevations of Archer's building appeared in *Vitruvius Britannicus*, and 1759, the date of Luke Sullivan's print, the

double stairs were added at the centre of the terrace in place of two separate stairs at each end.

In the portrait group by Philippe Mercier, the Prince is shown as a cellist in the company of his three eldest sisters. Certainly the centre of a rival 'political' court, the Prince seems to have also fostered an artistic and musical circle in opposition to the patronage of his parents, but these were never mutually exclusive. Music and politics combined in the most celebrated of the many entertainments held in the cliff-side theatre at Cliveden, on 1 August 1740: *The Masque of Alfred*, with words by the poets James Thomson and David Mallet and the Prince's secretary George, 1st Lord Lyttelton, and music by Thomas Arne: 'The whole was exhibited upon a Theatre in the Garden compos'd of vegetables, and decorated with Festoons of Flowers, at the End of which was erected a Pavillion for their Royal Highnesses ...', who were so delighted by the performance that they ordered a second the following night:

. . . with the addition of some favourite pantomime scenes from Mr Rich's Entertainments, which was accordingly begun, but the Rain falling very heavy, obliged them to break off before it was half over; upon which his Royal Highness commanded them to finish the Masque of Alfred in the House.[16]

Another commentator alleged that 'All the Common People were admitted, and were with most of the Performers made exceedingly Drunk'.[17]

Alfred has been shown to have combined the story of a British 'ruler in waiting' with many of the political ideas of Lord Bolingbroke's *The Idea of a Patriot King* (1738),[18] that is, a king who rules by consent rather than tyranny. This was also a central tenet of Lord Cobham's 'Boy Patriots', who met at just this time 40 miles away in the Temple of Friendship at Stowe (which was built in commemoration of Frederick's visit there in 1737) and whose number included Lyttelton, Cobham's nephew. The masque celebrated not only Alfred but all the other royal worthies included in Lord Cobham's Temple of British Worthies at Stowe (c.1735): the Black Prince, Queen Elizabeth and William III. The concluding climax of the piece was the first performance of the most patriotic ode in all British music:

The ruins of Cliveden after the 1795 fire; by Hendrick de Cort (collection Viscount Astor; photo courtesy Colnaghi's London)

When Britain first, at Heaven's command,
Arose from out the azure main,
This was the charter of the land,
And guardian angels sung this strain:
'Rule, Britannia, rule the waves;
Britons never will be slaves.'

It was apparently at Cliveden ten years later that the Patriot-King-in-waiting was struck a blow with a cricket ball while playing with his children, an injury which is thought to have caused his death, aged 44, in 1751.

After the Prince's death the Countess of Orkney and her husband Lord Inchiquin took Cliveden back in hand, but apparently continued to live mainly at Taplow Court. The Countess died in 1756, and her husband in 1777. The combined estates and the Orkney title passed to their only daughter Mary, who was deaf and dumb from birth. She in turn had married *her* first cousin, Murrough O'Brien in 1753, and he succeeded as 5th Earl of Inchiquin on the death of his uncle/father-in-law in 1777. It was the 5th Earl (later Marquess of Thomond) who employed 'Capability' Brown from *c.*1776, though it is not clear whether he was concerned with the Cliveden demesne as well as Taplow Court.[19]

Cliveden seems to have been used only occasionally towards the end of the century. The 2nd Countess died in 1791 and her daughter, the third successive Countess of Orkney in her own right, was living in the house as a widow when, on 20 May 1795, a careless servant knocked over a candle while turning down a bed, and the house caught fire. The diarist Caroline Lybbe Powys was among those who came to see the damaged house once the fire was out:

… the whole fabric, except one wing, a scene of ruin the flight of stone steps all fallen in pieces; but what

An early nineteenth-century drawing of the garden front records a proposed scheme for rebuilding Cliveden which was never executed (collection Viscount Astor)

seem'd the most unaccountable was, that the hall, which had fell in, and was a mass of stone pillars and bricks all in pieces, but two deal folding-doors not the least hurt, looking as if just fresh painted![20]

She added that 'very few articles of value were saved', and that Lady Orkney, who was living in one of the wings at the time of the visit (three months after the fire), had escaped 'without a rag'. The appearance of the ruined house is also recorded in a painting by Hendrick de Cort, exhibited at the Royal Academy in 1798 (illustrated on p.19).[21]

For some time the site of the ruined house stood empty. Though a widow, Lady Orkney seems to have entertained the idea of rebuilding at least twice. In 1813 she added a gothick summer-house to the 'neat fishing cottage' that stood by a popular mineral spring in the cliff just by the edge of the Thames, creating in effect a miniature spa. It was designed by the Scottish-born architect Peter Nicholson (1765–1844), who is better known for his many books on architecture and building crafts than for his surviving buildings. In 1816 he published an engraved design for rebuilding the ruined house in the castellated style.[22] A quite different,

perhaps slightly earlier, design from another hand survives in the form of a large, anonymous, worked-up perspective drawing for the south front.[23] This shows a more horizontal massing with the central block reduced to five bays from nine, linking wings in place of the colonnades, and the whole front set back from the line of the earlier house. The style of the drawing is close to the work of John Nash,[24] but the centrepiece, with its detached columns derived from the Arch of Constantine at Rome (and used by Adam for the north front of Kedleston in Derbyshire), closely anticipates the St Giles' elevation of the (much later) Ashmolean Museum at Oxford by C. R. Cockerell.[25]

Cliveden was advertised for sale by auction in 1818 but no sale seems to have taken place. It was again offered, this time successfully, in 1821, but because the property was devised under Lord Thomond's will to his great-grandson Thomas, Viscount Kirkwall, later 5th Earl of Orkney, conveyance to the new owner was delayed until Kirkwall's coming-of-age in 1824.

NOTES

1 See H. H. E. Cra'aster, ed., 'Letters of the First Lord Orkney during Marlborough's Campaigns', *English Historical Review*, xix, 1904, pp.307–21.

2 Ibid., p.320.

3 The prime set, still at Blenheim Palace, was woven *c*.1706; six further sets were woven for his generals: the others belonged to Lord Cobham at Stowe, to Lord Cadogan at Caversham in Surrey, to the Duke of Argyll at Inveraray in Argyllshire, to General Webb at Biddesden in Wiltshire, and to General Lumley at Stansted in Sussex. See Alan Wace, *The Marlborough Tapestries at Blenheim Palace*, London, 1968.

4 16 May 1710. *The Marlborough–Godolphin Correspondence*, ed. Henry Snyder, 1975, iii, p.1497.

5 Letter to Lady Mar, October 1727, in Robert Halsband, ed., *The Selected Letters of Lady Mary Wortley Montagu*, London, 1986, p.152.

6 NLS MS 1033.

7 NLS MS 1033, f.14–14A; 'burley' is Burley-on-the-Hill, Rutland, where a new house was built for Lord Nottingham in 1700–5, also replacing a former property of the 2nd Duke of Buckingham.

8 Cliveden Album, pp.43–4, and see Jackson-Stops in *Architectural History*, xix, 1976, p.6–7.

9 p.83.

10 S. Lewis, *Topographical Dictionary . . .*, iv, 1831, p.300.

11 Also James Gibbs, to whom unexecuted designs for the Octagon Temple on pp.39–40 of the Cliveden Album have been attributed. Gibbs's early career was supported by another of Orkney's fellow generals, the Duke of Argyll, whose English seat at Sudbrooke in Surrey he had designed in 1717, and who appointed him Architect of the Ordnance in 1727.

12 See Sir George Young, *The People's Prince*, 1937, and Joan Walters, *The Royal Griffin*, 1972.

13 Lady Archibald Hamilton served as Mistress of the Robes to the Princess. According to Hervey, she can also be numbered with the Prince's many mistresses.

14 1 October 1806: Kathryn Cave, ed., *The Diary of Joseph Farington*, London, 1982, viii, p.2871.

15 Quoted by Young, 1937, p.143.

16 *The London Daily Post and General Advertiser*, 5 August 1740, quoted in *Music and Letters*, October 1974, p.386.

17 Marchioness Grey, letter to Lady Mary Gregory, 12 August 1740. Bedfordshire Record Office, Lucas MSS L30/9A/1/p.1.

18 For this interpretation, see Michael Burden, 'A Mask for Politics: *The Masque of Alfred*', *The Music Review*, February 1988, pp.21–30.

19 Dorothy Stroud, *Capability Brown*, revised ed. 1975, p.182.

20 Emily J. Climenson, *Passages from the Diaries of Mrs Philip Lybbe Powys*, 1899, p.285.

21 Also in two naïve and anonymous watercolours: illus. *Country Life*, 24 February 1977, figs 12, 13.

22 Howard Colvin, *A Biographical Dictionary of British Architects 1600–1840*, 1978, p.594.

23 In the possession of Viscount Astor.

24 Gervase Jackson-Stops, *Country Life*, 24 February 1977, p.441.

25 A more recent use of the idea can be found at Pitzhanger, Ealing, designed by Sir John Soane for himself in 1800–3, but the Cliveden drawing has none of his characteristics; Cockerell did not begin to practise architecture until about 1818. His son Frederick Pepys Cockerell was responsible for the Italianate pavilion at the west end of the terrace at Cliveden in the 1860s.

CHAPTER THREE
VICTORIAN CLIVEDEN (1824–93)

Ye Guardian Spirits of these shades, rejoice!
Nymphs, Fauns, and Dryads join in grateful voice!
Hail the new Lord of this reclaimed domain,
Who bears no flaunting mistress in his train,
Nor sighs for former joys which revelled here,
When lust and riot led their mad career.

This anonymous piece of satirical doggerel in imitation of Pope, entitled 'On Sir G. W. Purchasing Clifden',[1] ends with an entreaty to the rats that inhabit the banks of Cliveden Reach:

With kindred welcome greet the Lord ye love;
For nibbling times and rich repasts prepare,
His ends, his parings, and his fame to share.

It must date from 1824, when at last Cliveden's new owner, Sir George Warrender, 4th baronet (1782–1849), completed his purchase.[2] He was the heir to a sizeable Edinburgh trading fortune, and a Member of Parliament. A man of somewhat legendary epicurean tastes (hence the expectant rats), he was nicknamed 'Sir Gorgeous Provender' by the wit Sydney Smith.

The particulars of sale first published in 1818 emphasised the survival of '... the foundation of the former noble Mansion (destroyed by fire about twenty years ago) composed of massive materials, and supposed to be equal to the reception of a new mansion equal in extent to the former.'[3] For his new mansion Sir George chose an Edinburgh architect, William Burn, who had recently worked for him at Lochend House in East Lothian but was then little known in England. The foundations of Lord Orkney's house (and the two wings, which survived entire) were a precise determinant of the outline of the new plans, which date from 1827.[4] Lochend had been Gothic, and the majority of Burn's later houses (of which there were a very great number, including Taplow Court, rebuilt for C. P. Grenfell in

1855–6) were variations of the 'Jacobethan' style and invariably very large. Burn's practice was still flourishing at his death in 1870, but even for an early work his Cliveden design was markedly restrained, more than respecting the early Georgian wings and itself resembling at first glance a house in the middle of the previous century.

The new house had only two storeys where Winde's had had four, reduced to three by Archer for Lord Orkney – a successive lowering that may have been due to the exposed site. With its loggia and *porte-cochère* on the north front, and a columned drawing-room on the terrace side occupying almost half the ground-floor area, the house was clearly intended primarily for entertainments. On Sir George's death in 1849, the house was again put up for sale.

From 1849 until 1893 Cliveden belonged successively to the two wealthiest families of the Victorian age, the Sutherlands and the Grosvenors. Though their architectural achievements can be considered as quite distinct phases of the history of the place,[5] in many other respects it was one continuous phase. The fortunes of both families rose to their peak under Victoria. Both added Cliveden to an already vast patrimony, using it as a retreat from London. Stafford House in St James's, the London 'palace' of the Sutherlands, and Grosvenor House in Park Lane were the two most magnificent town houses of their time. Both families had great houses in the North-West – Trentham and Eaton – and both had extensive interests in the Highlands of Scotland.

Above all they were closely related, in some cases twice over. In 1852 Hugh Lupus, Earl Grosvenor (later 1st Duke of Westminster) married his first cousin Lady Constance Leveson-Gower; when he purchased Cliveden seventeen years later he was buying from the estate of his mother-in-law and

The interior of Stafford House, the Sutherlands' London home; by James Wingfield (detail)

aunt by marriage what had been one of his wife's childhood homes, and so it was almost as if he was succeeding to the property by inheritance. The many strands of kinship between the families meant that many of the Sutherlands' regular guests continued to come to Cliveden as regularly to stay with the Grosvenors.

A further strand of continuity was the Queen herself. Harriet, Duchess of Sutherland was appointed Mistress of the Robes at the coronation in 1837 and held the post almost without interruption until 1861. She was the Queen's devoted friend, and of all her children the Queen's favourite was Lady Constance. The Queen's close interest in Cliveden and its families therefore endured from the purchase of the estate by the Sutherlands in 1849 to its sale by the Duke of Westminster in 1893.

The dukedom of Sutherland, created in 1833, concluded a steady accumulation of titles and landed estates through three centuries, beginning with those of the Gowers of Yorkshire, which were joined in the mid-seventeenth century with the Staffordshire property of the Levesons (at which time the family name became Leveson-Gower, pronounced 'Looson-Gore'). In the eighteenth century there began what Disraeli called the family's 'talent for absorbing heiresses'; in 1748 Granville Leveson-Gower (1721–1803), 2nd Earl Gower, married Louisa Egerton, sister and heiress of the 'Canal' 3rd Duke of Bridgewater, and in 1785 their son George Granville Leveson-Gower (1758–1833), Viscount Trentham, married Elizabeth, Countess of Sutherland in her own right, the 19th of that line and the beneficiary of a disputed succession to about a million acres. These marriages eventually brought on the one hand the rising incomes of coal mines in Staffordshire and Lancashire, and the country's first great canals built by the Duke of Bridgewater, and on the other, the greater part of the county of Sutherland. The 2nd Earl achieved some distinction in Parliament and in public office, earning from Pitt the further title of Marquess of Stafford in 1786, but his son's greatest achievement was undoubtedly his marriage. Lord Ronald Gower conceded that his forebears had been 'more distinguished by their luck and by their alliances than in the senate or in the field'.

When the 1st Marquess died in 1803, in the same year as the great Duke of Bridgewater, the Stafford estates and titles passed to his eldest son, George, but the Bridgewater inheritance was put in trust, to pass on George's death (in 1833) to his second son, Lord Francis (1800–57), who also assumed the Bridgewater name of Egerton in place of Leveson-Gower.

Lady Sutherland's family had been seated at Dunrobin Castle in Sutherland, on the east coast of Scotland above the Firth of Dornoch, since the early fifteenth century. At the time of her marriage in 1785 her vast estates were producing a negligible rental income; when outgoings such as poor relief were accounted for, they were running at a deficit. When her husband inherited the Stafford fortunes in 1803, there began a process whereby capital from the family's industrial concerns in Staffordshire and Lancashire was diverted northwards to reverse decades of neglectful management. From 1812 this exercise in 'improvement' on the grandest scale was entrusted to James Loch, an Edinburgh lawyer and intellectual who as estate superintendent was to be 'the major instrument in the direction of the economic policies of the family' until his death in 1855.[6]

The strategy for improving the Highland estates was already in place when Loch took over. It was the wholesale removal of the impoverished population, whose system of subsistence farming was not thought susceptible to improvement, to new settlements in the coastal regions where profitable agriculture could develop; many were also driven to emigrate at this time. Whatever the theoretical arguments in its favour, the over-zealous way in which the policy was put into effect by some of Loch's agents and factors was to engender bitter resentment and condemnation (including an essay by Karl Marx, *Sutherland and Slavery*, in 1853).

Meanwhile the combined inheritance of the Stafford and Bridgewater estates in England left the family holding the balance of power in the greatest economic struggle of the Industrial Revolution, between the ascendant system of canals and the emerging phenomenon of the railways. By 1826 Lord Stafford was probably the largest proprietor on both sides.[7]

George, 2nd Duke of Sutherland (1786–1861);
by Sir Thomas Lawrence (Dunrobin Castle)

In January 1827 the King's brother, the Duke of York, died, leaving unfinished a palatial house which was being built for him on the Mall in London to designs by Benjamin Dean Wyatt (with his brother Philip). The finance for what was to have been called York House seems to have been lent by Lord Stafford, and in December the same year he acquired it on a long lease for £72,000, as a London home for his eldest son, Lord Gower. Lord Stafford christened it Stafford House and retained the services of the Wyatts to complete the work, somewhat to the irritation of Lord Gower and his young wife.

George Granville Leveson-Gower (1786–1861), 4th Earl Gower, had for some years been urged towards marriage by his father and by James Loch (anxious to secure the succession of the Sutherland/Stafford estates independent of the Bridgewater Trust) when at the age of 37 he succumbed to the charms of his seventeen-year-old cousin Lady Harriet Howard (1806–68), third daughter of the 6th Earl of Carlisle. He lost no more time, as Lady Carlisle's diary for 1823 records:

Friday April 25. My Brother's Ball for Harriet. Tuesday April 29. Hope of Lord Gower. Thursday May 1. Lord Gower's note. Esterhazy's Ball. Friday May 2. Lord Gower proposed and was accepted.[8]

Lord Gower's career as a diplomat had been cut short by illness, and chronic deafness excluded him from public office. His adult life was devoted to his estates and enterprises, his family and, in partnership with his wife, the building or rebuilding of great houses. Lady Gower had been brought up at Castle Howard in Yorkshire and, as a granddaughter of the Duke of Devonshire, had often visited Chatsworth as a child. The first building project she was to undertake with her husband (1826–30) was at Lilleshall, the Shropshire house of the Levesons which had been given to the young couple by Lord Stafford.

In early 1833, at the age of 75, Lord Stafford was created Duke of Sutherland (his wife would thereafter be known as the Duchess-Countess). It was a title he enjoyed for only a few months, for in July of that year he died at Dunrobin. Perhaps with some exaggeration Lord Ronald Gower relates that 'almost the entire male population of the county' joined the funeral procession to Dornoch Cathedral. The Duke's statue by Francis Chantrey was raised on a 100-foot pedestal on the summit of Ben Bragghie, itself 1,300 feet above the castle and visible for many miles.

Before the year was out, the 2nd Duke and his wife had turned their attention to Trentham in Staffordshire, another Leveson house which had been remodelled by 'Capability' Brown and Henry Holland for the 1st Earl Gower. Although Brown had also landscaped the park, it was with a view to reintroducing a formal garden that the Duchess invited Charles Barry to survey the grounds that October. Barry progressed within a matter of months to proposals for the wholesale reshaping of the house, with the object of improving its layout as well as marking the new ducal rank of Staffordshire's greatest family. Work began in March 1834 at an estimated cost of £40,000.

While the work at Trentham was in progress, the Duke and Duchess were planning the completion of Stafford House, which, though largely built, was not finished internally. Again they turned to Barry,

The south front and Italian garden of Trentham in Staffordshire in 1900. Barry redesigned the garden and rebuilt the house for the Sutherlands

who began work on the staircase hall in 1838. Decorated in Louis XIV style, it was to be not just the grandest of any London house but one of the grandest in Europe (see p.23).

From his position as 'chancellor' in the 'kingdom' of the House of Sutherland James Loch took a long-term view. He clung to the principle that capital should remain inviolate and that expenditure must consequently be kept within earnings. During the 1830s he began to issue warnings of a trend in the opposite direction. Not only was the expense of building works at Trentham and Stafford House having to be met from capital, but it was inevitable that the effect of the increased annual expenditure on their upkeep would be to put the revenue account permanently into debt. 'Let me beg you to keep your architects in order,' he had written to the Duke in 1835, '... I am quite sure they do not think it a matter of much importance [to keep within estimates].'[9] Barry's initial estimate of £40,000 at Trentham had become £72,000 by 1840, but far from bringing work to a halt the Duke authorised a

further phase; by the end of 1841 he had spent £123,000. Loch's prognosis was right: in 1842 the Duke spent £40,000 more than he earned, a deficit that had to be made good through land sales.

It is unlikely that Loch drew much comfort from the fact that it was not until work was complete at Stafford House that the Duke and Duchess summoned their architect to Dunrobin. Here he was engaged from 1844 to 1848 in transforming the ancient castle into a baronial fantasy worthy of Walt Disney. By 1848 this work had cost £41,400; at last the Duke had begun to hearken to Loch's entreaties and agreed to forego the extra expense of granite chimney-pieces. The occasion for their last and greatest project was an unforeseen calamity.

In 1849 the Duke of Sutherland conceived the idea of buying Cliveden for his wife as a retreat from London, and that April he had it surveyed. The estate was valued at £24,850 excluding standing timber, and with the house there was offered a

(Right) Harriet, Duchess of Sutherland (1805–68); painted by Franz Winterhalter in 1849, the year the Sutherlands bought Cliveden. She stands in the staircase hall of Stafford House, which had been redecorated by Charles Barry (Dunrobin Castle)

collection of furniture, pictures and effects worth a further £9,566. Needless to add, Loch was against what he regarded as an 'unproductive' purchase. Somehow the necessary £30,000 was identified and the sale was agreed. As early as June the family gathered at Cliveden to celebrate the marriage of the Duke's eldest son Lord Albert.

Cliveden was to belong to the Duchess, and any improvements were to be charged to her account, with the generous proviso that if she ran out of money she was entitled to borrow from her husband, the debt being entered on his. The house was only 25 years old and in good order, but the Duchess began a few internal alterations, which proceeded during the late summer and autumn.

Thursday, 15 November 1849 was declared a day of national thanksgiving for the ending of an epidemic of cholera which had killed 13,000 Londoners between June and October. While the Cliveden staff were at church that morning, a fire broke out in the heart of the house and quickly took hold. One of the first to notice it was the Queen, who saw the smoke rising in the distance as she came from the chapel at Windsor. (Another was a Mrs Blaine of Maidenhead, who – Ronald Gower discovered – 'happened to see both fires, that of 1795 and that of 1849, from, I believe, the same window

of the same house'.)[10] The Queen sent fire engines from the castle, and the neighbouring gentry teams of estate workers, but they could not save the main house, which was gutted. All hands were pressed into pulling down the connecting colonnades to prevent the fire spreading to the wings.

The blame for this disaster was immediately assumed to lie in some negligence on the part of the decorators. Within a week Charles Barry had been brought in to investigate and his report concluded that poor workmanship in the building of the house had been the true cause. Although iron beams had been used for the main structure of William Burn's house, the end of a wooden joist supporting the library floor had been left protruding into a chimney flue serving the servants' hall below. It had become overheated and set alight, and as soon as the flames had travelled the short distance to the fitted bookcases ('rich in fine editions of the French classics', according to Ronald Gower), they gained in ferocity.

The Duke's reaction was remarkable. He was exasperated that the fire had not been detected sooner; although it was a thanksgiving day, he would have expected the contractor to have been present. Beyond that he regretted the loss of the books and many of his wife's papers from the

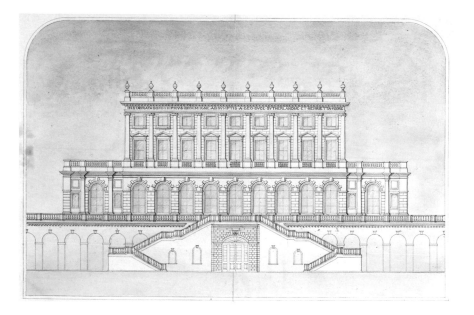

Barry's design for the centre of the garden front (collection Viscount Astor)

The garden front

library, but what moved him more than the news of the fire itself was 'the account of the prompt and kind exertions of the neighbourhood'. In a letter to Loch in response to the news, written from Scotland the day after the event, he refers to the weather and the walks he has been taking.[11]

The fire had come so soon after the purchase that the question of insurance was at first far from clear. No premium had been paid. With some relief the Duke's secretary was informed on the 17th that the loss was covered, and plans for rebuilding could be put in hand.

Despite the limitations of both style and site imposed by the survival of Archer's two wings, the rebuilding of Cliveden is undoubtedly among Barry's finest achievements. Taking as his starting point the outline of the old house as illustrated in *Vitruvius Britannicus* (see p.11), with its roof concealed by a heavy parapet lined with urns, Barry produced a synthesis of English Palladian architecture with the Roman Cinquecento. The result is close to, and follows on from, his remodelling of the south front of Harewood in Yorkshire seven years earlier, when (in order to add an extra storey) he removed Carr of York's portico and introduced a continuous order of giant pilasters supporting a heavy balustraded cornice. The similarity of the garden front of Cliveden and the Villa Albani was remarked on at the time, but even more apparent here and at Harewood is his debt to the famous Gallery at Somerset House, built in 1662 by John Webb, though long attributed to Inigo Jones. For one of the main façades at Trentham, Barry had closely followed that of Jones's Banqueting House in Whitehall, and these seventeenth-century influences may explain why the south front fully lives up to the grandeur of Winde's terrace.

A compact plan was possible since Cliveden was only for occasional use, yet Barry managed to provide valuable extra accommodation by the one-storey appendages built either side of the garden front. These were concealed from the court on the north side by the curving corridors to the wings, a free adaptation of Archer's open colonnades. The Gibbsian arched window surrounds and rusticated walls of the ground floor give a firm base to the two upper floors, which are decorated with Ionic pilasters and seem to be (though they are not) a *piano nobile*. On the garden side, the arches of the ground-floor windows also provide a subtle link between the new house and the great seventeenth-century terrace on which it stands.

According to his son and biographer, the Rev. Alfred Barry, the architect's preferred design had no pilasters, but had towers raised at each corner. In another preliminary design, Barry proposed three-quarter columns, doubled at each end, and with the entablature breaking forward over each, to produce a far more restless Baroque effect. In the end single pilasters were chosen to support a deep frieze, in which was carved a resounding Latin inscription, composed by Mr Gladstone, who was a close friend of the Sutherlands. On the north front he recorded the Duke of Buckingham's first house on this site, on the south the Duke and Duchess of Sutherland's later rebuilding, and on the west their debt to the 'Ingenio Opera Consilio Caroli Barry Archit'.

The exterior was entirely rendered in Roman cement on a base of brick, with the capitals, consoles, balusters and other dressings expressed in moulded terracotta supplied by M. H. Blanchard, who had been an apprentice in the firm of Coade & Sealy before setting up his own works in 1839. One of the Ionic pilaster capitals for Cliveden was exhibited on his stand at the Great Exhibition in 1851.[12] Blanchard also supplied the generous finials for the crowning balustrades (recalling Archer's), and terracotta 'baskets' for the lower ones, designs from a repertoire of vases, urns and other ornaments which Barry had developed to great effect at Trentham, and which here at Cliveden included stone urns sprouting bronze aloes. For the roof, which seems always to have been meant as a viewing platform (recalling the late seventeenth-century house), Barry's innovative design employed large slabs of Penrhyn slate laid on slate joists. The demolition of the ruined house began in the early months of 1850; Barry's drawings are mainly dated in the following year, and the house was ready for another wedding, that of Lady Constance Leveson-Gower and Hugh, Earl Grosvenor, in April 1852 when 200 guests attended a ball. The accounts of the main contractor, Lucas of Norwich, for 1850–1 alone amount to £25,000,[13] but the total cost (of which it seems only £11,400 was recovered in insurance) must have been far greater.

The decoration and furnishing of the new house continued until 1855. The entrance hall was paved

The west end of the Drawing Room, as designed by Barry. The doors lead to the Breakfast Room

The staircase ceiling, painted by A. L. Hervieu, who included portraits of the Duchess of Sutherland's children as the seasons. It is almost the only surviving element of her decorative schemes. The ornamental surround was added by J. D. Crace (see p.41)

with encaustic tiles in a concentric pattern resembling an antique mosaic, the most generous of many gifts from Herbert Minton, whose firm had recently tiled the Grand Corridor at Osborne in a similar style for the Queen and Prince Consort.[14] The Sutherlands were important patrons of the firm of Minton of Stoke-on-Trent and the Duchess undoubtedly influenced the course of the factory's designs.[15] According to her granddaughter Lady Frances Balfour, the Duchess '... inculcated the exact imitation of wild flowers on breakfast services',[16] and this 'naturalism' was the hallmark of her taste in decoration generally. At Cliveden the new library bookcases were designated not in the usual way with numbers, but by the names of plants carved in sycamore on each press.[17]

For ceilings the Duchess employed the firm of Morant & Boyd, which had worked for the Duke of Bedford. In the cove of her own sitting-room or 'boudoir' in the south-east corner of the ground floor, the portraits of her grandchildren by the French *émigré* A. L. Hervieu were reserved in ovals within a dense floral trellis, more of which covered the ceiling of the Dining Room at the opposite end

of the house. Here, Morant's painting was deemed so true to nature that '... the peaches, grapes, figs and pomegranates seem ready to fall on the floor.'[18] The Duchess's own portrait and that of her mother-in-law, the Duchess-Countess, appeared among the treillage of the Drawing Room ceiling. Hervieu also painted the Duchess's children in the guise of the four seasons on the ceiling of the staircase (almost the only feature of all this work that survives today) and in her boudoir, a large panel of *The Judgement of Paris*, in which only two of the three goddesses were represented. Paris was seen to offer the golden apple out of the frame, implying the presence in the room itself of the third and victorious goddess, Venus.[19] A more sober note was struck by Barry's chimney-pieces, in 'statuary veined St Anne's and Griotte [marbles]'.

At the time of the fire, much of the ground-floor furniture had been moved out of the way of the workmen and was stored in the Billiard Room and so escaped destruction, but nothing survived from the library or the upper floors. This was replaced in 1853–4 by purchases from Gillow, Hindley & Trollope, but the most costly furniture for the new

*Cliveden ferry,
with Ferry Cottage
beyond; photograph
by Henry Taunt,
c.1883*

house came from Paris and was supplied by Morin, to whom £2,355 was paid in 1854–5.[20]

The best pictures were always kept in London. At Cliveden, to judge from a list of those removed on the Duchess's death in 1868,[21] they were largely by contemporary artists. There were the Winterhalters: of the Duchess herself (the version in oils that remains at Cliveden, and several coloured prints of the prime full-length in other rooms) and a posthumous likeness of the infant daughter Aline, who had died in 1849 aged only one. (A portrait of Lady Constance was commissioned by the Queen and has always been at Windsor.) The stairs were hung with sixteen views of Italy commissioned from William Leighton Leitch, who had instructed the Queen in watercolour.

Sculpture played an important part in the interior of the house as well as in the embellishment of the grounds (see Chapter Six). In the library were Carrier-Belleuse's bronze statuettes of Lord Albert and Lord Ronald, and John Graham Lough's *Ariel* stood in the Drawing Room. The bronze of *Joan of Arc* by the Princesse Marie d'Orléans (see p.83) had pride of place in the Hall, which became one of the grounds for the falling-out between architect and

client in 1855. For some years Barry had been losing money on the Houses of Parliament, and in a letter to Loch in January that year, he claimed that, with the exception of his fee (5%) on the Cliveden rebuilding contract, he had not been paid by the Duke since 1848. He submitted an account. The Duke reacted to Loch:

Sir C. Barry [he had been knighted in 1852] has taken me by surprise . . . Journeys and travelling expenses [to Cliveden] £105.6.0!!! – in a coach and four one would suppose – Arrangement of Statues! . . . what statues he has had to place I do not know – there is one in the Hall of Joan of Arc – the choice of place seems more expensive than the cost of the statue – if the charges were not so provoking they would be ridiculous.[22]

The Duke settled the matter by paying the account in full but making it clear that if ever Sir Charles should call, the porter had instructions not to admit him.

At Trentham, Barry had progressed from garden to mansion to stables, and eventually to cottages and out-offices. At Cliveden it may be that the architect of the Houses of Parliament would have had nothing to do with these latter necessities,[23] but in any case a replacement was needed. The choice of

George Devey, who seems first to have worked at Cliveden in 1857, was an inspired one; he was to make a speciality of designing cottages in the vernacular and the six he built at Cliveden (as well as a dairy and a boathouse) are among his most successful. The first of them, Spring Cottage (1857), was an adaptation – the further extension of the cottage gothicised for the Countess of Orkney in 1813, but the rest were entirely his own.[24]

In 1857 another new architect, Henry Clutton, was called in to design a new set of offices. Three years later a report was sent to George Loch, who had by now succeeded his father James, to the effect that the domestic water system at Cliveden was unsatisfactory. The water supply for the mansion came from an artesian well at White Place, a model farm on the other side of the Thames. It was pumped under the river bed and up to the house in a glazed pipe. In the guise of a campanile or clock-tower there now rose under Clutton's direction a 100-foot *water* tower (holding 17,000 gallons and still in use), completed in 1861 at a cost of £3,000. Though executed by Clutton, its design was based directly on Barry's tower at Trentham, built twenty years earlier.

A photograph by Henry Taunt which probably dates from the 1870s suggests that from its origins in practical necessity the clock-tower became a monument to the 2nd Duke, since the date of his death, 28 February 1861, appears in the pediments on the visible sides. He had suffered a fit of paralysis early in January at Trentham, where the family had spent Christmas, and never recovered. An over-life-size statue of his standing figure, commissioned by his widow from Matthew Noble, was set up on the main south axis at Cliveden (in 1866 his son, the 3rd Duke, placed an identical bronze on the main axis at Dunrobin – see p.57).

Shortly after succeeding to the dukedom in 1833 the 2nd Duke had written to his mother, 'We are all so well off that there can be no cause of uneasiness in any respect to any of our worldly goods, of which there is such a plentiful abundance.' He managed to retain this equanimity in the face of his much younger and more talented wife's building-mania for nearly 30 years; only latterly did he weaken somewhat before Loch's persistent disapproval,

admitting in 1850 that he wished Stafford House had burnt down and not Cliveden: the saving in running costs would have been great.[25]

The widowed Duchess had Cliveden as her jointure house. She was also given the use of Chiswick House by the Duke of Devonshire (who was both her cousin and brother-in-law), but continued to entertain important guests at Cliveden during the years that remained before her own death in 1868, among them Alfred Tennyson, the Gladstones, Sir Joseph Paxton and the sculptor Marochetti. Gladstone's niece Lucy Cavendish was a visitor in June 1863: 'The perfect taste, refinement, and luxury of the place almost oppresses me. When one lives in Paradise, how hard it must be to ascend in heart and mind to Heaven!'[26] The Queen herself was lent the house when, at the height of the political crisis surrounding the passage of Gladstone's Reform Bill in the early summer of 1866, she had felt it unwise to be as far away as Balmoral.[27] But the most celebrated visitor of all in this time was Giuseppe Garibaldi.

Henry Clutton's water-tower, photographed shortly after it was completed in 1861

Garibaldi was invited to England in April 1864 by the 3rd Duke of Sutherland, whose wife was considered daringly radical for an aristocrat and had made Stafford House a Liberal salon. The visit caused a sensation, recalled twenty years later by Ronald Gower:

April 11 was the day of Garibaldi's reception in London ... Up to seven in the evening the entrance side of Stafford House was packed with a dense crowd which extended into the Green Park ... Pall Mall was impassable.

Approaching the *porte-cochère* the general's carriage practically disintegrated from the weight of the mob clinging on. After ten days in London, including a visit to the Duchess at Chiswick, Garibaldi was to have made a tour about the country but this was abandoned, most probably for the sake of his health. Before his departure he stayed with the Duchess at Cliveden (in a room on the ground floor which for some years was kept as he left it and known as the Garibaldi Room). He was delighted with the grounds, declaring that the view of the Thames from his terrace room recalled some of the mighty river prospects of South America.[28]

Duchess Harriet died in 1868. Her son, the 3rd Duke, had no use for Cliveden, which was purchased from her estate by her son-in-law, Hugh Lupus, Earl Grosvenor (1825–99). For Lord Grosvenor there were practical as well as sentimental reasons for the acquisition of the house in which he and his wife had spent their honeymoon in 1852. For the heir to a family tradition on the Turf and in the hunting field, there were advantages in a house so close to Ascot. Besides, for most of the ten years from October 1869, when he inherited a marquessate and an income of over £150,000, Cliveden was his only habitable English country house. Throughout the 1870s, the new Marquess was engaged in rebuilding his principal house, Eaton in Cheshire. Designed by Alfred Waterhouse and completed at a cost of £600,000, it remained the epitome of the High Victorian country house until its demolition in 1961–3.[29]

Grosvenor had been elected to Parliament as a member for Chester in 1847, but had not been closely involved in national politics until the 1866

crisis. Gladstone was later to acknowledge that Grosvenor (his friend and neighbour – their estates abutted each other on the Flint/Cheshire border) had 'taken the chief part' in destroying his 1866 Reform Bill. From that time until his death in 1899, Grosvenor was to remain prominent in public life, especially after his elevation to a dukedom in Gladstone's Dissolution Honours of 1874. His causes included the improvement of agriculture, the welfare of shop assistants, gardeners and other working people, and the preservation of the countryside. On his death *The Times* noted that in these years he 'could pass from the racecourse to a missionary

Hugh Lupus, 1st Duke of Westminster (1825–99), who bought Cliveden from his wife's family in 1868; by J. E. Millais, 1872 (Eaton Hall, Cheshire)

R. W. Edis's design for remodelling the east (guest) wing in Flemish Renaissance style. Only this part of his scheme was executed and it was later demolished by the Astors

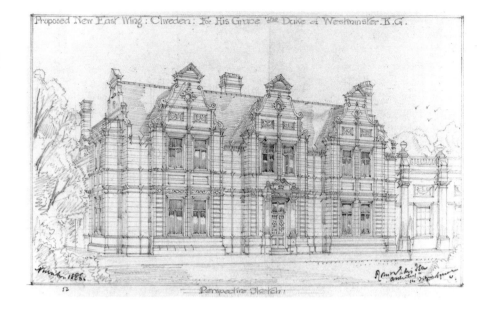

meeting without incurring the censure of the strictest.'[30]

An estimate dated 24 December 1869 lists the immediate improvements Lord Westminster deemed necessary at Cliveden: a *porte-cochère* to the main entrance on the north front, new stables, and the re-ordering of the *cour d'honneur* between the two wings and the Grand Avenue. There were also alterations to be made in the heating of the house and in the domestic offices. The architect was again Clutton, and most of his external works remain as completed in 1870.[31] Clutton was simultaneously employed in the complete remodelling of the state rooms at Grosvenor House in Park Lane, but his only structural contribution to the interior of Cliveden was the combining of Barry's two drawing-rooms on the south front. It was in Clutton's new rooms at Grosvenor House, hung with outstanding pictures by Rubens, Velázquez and Rembrandt, Reynolds's *Mrs Siddons* and Gainsborough's *Blue Boy*, that the Westminsters held their greatest entertainments.

In 1879 the Duchess fell ill with Bright's disease. She was well enough to see her husband's horse Bend' Or win the Derby the following year, but after catching a chill, her condition worsened. The Queen visited her at Grosvenor House, finding her 'paler and her voice much weaker. She reminded me so much of her dear mother.' After a spell at Cliveden she was taken on doctors' instructions to Bournemouth. She died there in December 1880, aged only 45. In 1882 the Duke took as his second wife the 24-year old Katherine, youngest daughter of his friend Lord Chesham. Their life was based at Eaton, where the Duke had begun in earnest to develop the stud that was to produce another three Derby winners before the end of the century. He made one further significant contribution to Cliveden.

In the mid-1880s the Duke commissioned designs from R. W. (later Sir Robert) Edis for the wholesale remodelling of the two wings in the style of the Flemish Renaissance.[32] Edis's first drawing, dated November 1886, was for the east (guest) wing only; it was followed, in July 1888, by a scheme to restore symmetry to the forecourt by a similar treatment on the west side, but only the first of the proposals was ever executed. One of W. W. Astor's first acts on purchasing Cliveden from the Duke in 1893 was to demolish this 'Tudor' aberration, whose appearance cannot have been improved by a surface of 'pink stucco',[33] and to return the wing to its appearance much as Barry had left it.

With his London estates alone yielding an income

of £250,000, the Duke was almost certainly the richest Englishman of his day, but in June 1893 he decided that the growing expense of his two families and his charitable commitments dictated some retrenchment. He decided to sell Cliveden to an American millionaire, William Waldorf Astor. When the Queen heard the news she wrote at once from Italy:

[She was] deeply grieved to read of … the necessity the Duke feels himself under of selling dear beautiful Cliveden … The Duke must excuse the Queen if she says she thinks he has built too much at Eaton … The Queen is however glad he thinks that at any rate the beauties and quiet of the place will be preserved, but it is grievous to think of it falling into these hands![34]

In the same year the Duke's name appeared at the head of a list of members of a 'provisional Council' whose aim was the establishment of the National Trust.

NOTES

1 Newspaper cutting, Cliveden Album, p.108a.

2 The price of £39,500, as reported in *The Times* on 14 Nov. 1818, was rather more than the Duke of Sutherland was to pay in 1849.

3 Cliveden Album, p.56b.

4 RIBA Arc.III, 63–8.

5 Even this distinction is somewhat blurred, since the architects Henry Clutton and George Devey, and the head gardener John Fleming all worked for both families.

6 Eric Richards, *The Leviathan of Wealth: The Sutherland Fortune in the Industrial Revolution*, 1973, p.19.

7 Ibid., p.39.

8 Quoted in Lady Leconfield, ed., *The Three Howard Sisters*, 1975, p.17.

9 Staffordshire Record Office (SRO): Loch to Sutherland 27/2/1835.

10 *Reminiscences*, i, p.15n.

11 SRO D593 K/1/3/37, 16 November 1849.

12 *The Builder*, x, 1852.

13 SRO D593 K/1/10/8.

14 See Joan Jones, *Minton, The First Two Hundred Years of Design and Production*, 1993, p.170. A frieze of Minton tiles which Barry incorporated in the staircase decoration does not survive.

15 See Philip Ward-Jackson, 'A.-E. Carrier-Belleuse, J.-J. Feuchère and the Sutherlands', *Burlington Magazine*, March 1985. Examples of maiolica and other wares were lent by the Duke for reproduction by Minton, and even the water supply for the factory came from the Trentham estate. Parian figures or busts of Lady Constance, Lord Albert and Lord Ronald Leveson-Gower were modelled for Minton by Carrier-Belleuse, and busts of the Duke and Duchess by Matthew Noble.

16 Lady Frances Balfour, *Ne Obliviscaris*, 1930, p.226.

17 *Liverpool Mercury*, April 1852.

18 Gower, *Reminiscences*, i, p.28.

19 Newspaper cutting, 1864.

20 SRO D593 R/1/15/7.

21 SRO D593 R/3/2/9/14.

22 SRO D593 K/1/3/43, 18 January 1855.

23 Barry evidently carried out *some* peripheral work. The screen walls flanking the Windsor or Laundry gate (enclosing Devey's lodge) are clearly his, and a drawing for them among the Sutherland papers at Stafford (D593 H/12/5/15/1), though unsigned, is attributable to him.

24 Woodgate Cottage in 1857, Windsor and Taplow Lodges around the same time, and Ferry Cottage in 1861. The house now known as Seven Gables was built in 1879 for the Duke of Westminster. See Jill Allibone, *George Devey*, 1991, pp.46–7, 153.

25 SRO Sutherland to Loch, 21/2/1850.

26 John Bailey, ed., *The Diary of Lady Frederick Cavendish*, London, 1927, i, p.162.

27 It may have been in gratitude for this particular kindness that the Queen sent an electrotype copy of a marble statue of her husband by William Theed (see p.84). According to a tradition retailed by the 2nd Lord Astor, the house was occupied by 89 people, including staff, during the Queen's sojourn.

28 Gower, *Reminiscences*, i, p.20.

29 It has since been twice replaced.

30 Quoted in Gervas Huxley, *Victorian Duke*, 1967, p.xii.

31 Gervase Jackson-Stops, 'The Cliveden Album II', *Architectural History*, 1977, pp.70–1 and notes.

32 Cliveden Album, pp.46, 76.

33 Typescript notes by 1st Viscount Astor, *c*.1920, in possession of Viscount Astor.

34 Quoted in Huxley, op. cit., p.141.

FAMILY TREE OF THE LEVESON-GOWERS
AND THE GROSVENORS

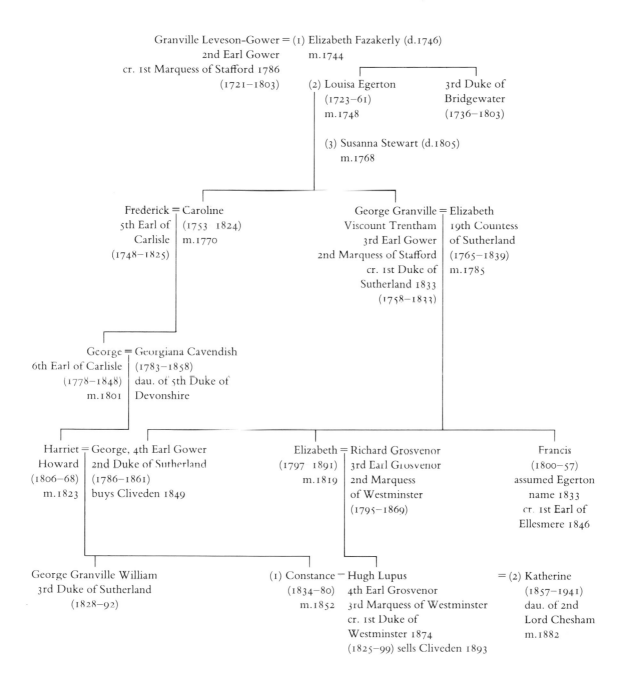

Granville Leveson-Gower = (1) Elizabeth Fazakerly (d.1746)
2nd Earl Gower   m.1744
cr. 1st Marquess of Stafford 1786
(1721–1803)

(2) Louisa Egerton   3rd Duke of
(1723–61)   Bridgewater
m.1748   (1736–1803)

(3) Susanna Stewart (d.1805)
m.1768

Frederick = Caroline   George Granville = Elizabeth
5th Earl of (1753–1824)   Viscount Trentham 19th Countess
Carlisle   m.1770   3rd Earl Gower   of Sutherland
(1748–1825)   2nd Marquess of Stafford (1765–1839)
                                 cr. 1st Duke of   m.1785
                                 Sutherland 1833
                                 (1758–1833)

George = Georgiana Cavendish
6th Earl of Carlisle (1783–1858)
(1778–1848)   dau. of 5th Duke of
m.1801   Devonshire

Harriet = George, 4th Earl Gower   Elizabeth = Richard Grosvenor   Francis
Howard   2nd Duke of Sutherland   (1797–1891) 3rd Earl Grosvenor   (1800–57)
(1806–68) (1786–1861)   m.1819   2nd Marquess   assumed Egerton
m.1823   buys Cliveden 1849   of Westminster   name 1833
                                                   (1795–1869)   cr. 1st Earl of
                                                                         Ellesmere 1846

George Granville William   (1) Constance — Hugh Lupus   = (2) Katherine
3rd Duke of Sutherland   (1834–80)   4th Earl Grosvenor   (1857–1941)
(1828–92)   m.1852   3rd Marquess of Westminster dau. of 2nd
                                               cr. 1st Duke of   Lord Chesham
                                               Westminster 1874   m.1882
                                               (1825–99) sells Cliveden 1893

William Waldorf, 1st Viscount Astor (1848–1919), who bought Cliveden in 1893; by Hubert von Herkomer (Dining Room)

CHAPTER FOUR
THE ASTORS (1893–1966)

By the time he purchased Cliveden in 1893 William Waldorf Astor (1848–1919), the heir to an immense American fortune, had reverted entirely to his family's European roots. 'America is good enough for any man who has to make a livelihood,' he declared, 'though why travelled people of independent means should remain there more than a week is not readily to be comprehended'.[1] His great-grandfather John Jacob Astor I had left the village of Walldorf in Germany as a younger son aged twenty in 1783, travelling to America after a short stay in London. Settling in New York he found work with a fur trader, and before long set himself up in the same business. By the 1830s he had become a pillar of New York society, owner of the American Fur Company and the Pacific Fur Company, the greatest trading concerns on the continent, and substantial property investments in New York.

William Waldorf was the only child of John Jacob Astor III and his wife Charlotte Augusta Gibbs. After a private education and law school, he decided to enter State politics, becoming a member of the State Senate in 1879. Two years later he stood for election to Congress, but was defeated after an acrimonious campaign. He had married Mary Dahlgren Paul in 1878, and in 1882 they embarked for Europe, where Astor took up the appointment of US Minister in Rome. As his grandson has written, from this decisive moment his life acquired 'a pattern of formalistic behaviour which fell somewhere between that of a Roman emperor and his idea of an English medieval baron.'[2] He began to collect ancient sculpture, medieval and Renaissance works of art, and Old Master pictures, and became acquainted with artists then working in Rome, notably William Wetmore Story, who apparently gave him some instruction in sculpture (see p.59). He extended his historical explorations with ventures into fiction, publishing two novels (*Valentino*

and *Sforza*) and a book of short stories (*Pharaoh's Daughter*) in the 1880s.

It is not hard to understand the appeal Cliveden must have exerted on such a man when it became available in 1893. Here was a villa on the pattern of those with which he had become fondly familiar during the ten years of his diplomatic duties in Rome (he had one of his own, near Sorrento), but which could also offer rich associations with English history. At the same time as buying Cliveden, he took a lease of Lansdowne House and purchased premises on Victoria Embankment as a London office. He also began his family's association with the British press with the purchase in 1892 of the *Pall Mall Gazette*.[3]

Tragically, only a year after these purchases his wife Mary died, and he set about the task of restoring Cliveden, which he took on in a somewhat dilapidated state, on his own. He planned a programme of repairs and improvements that began in 1895. One of his first requirements was privacy, and he rapidly completed the perimeter wall of the estate. This naturally fuelled local suspicions of the new American proprietor: 'Waldorf by name and walled-off by nature.'[4]

Astor's many embellishments and additions are described in his notes compiled about 1905 and typed up in 1920 after his death, and were, almost without exception, a success. He began by reversing the Duke of Westminster's aberrant recasting of the east wing in the 'Tudor' style, returning it almost exactly to Barry's design. Next, he called on the architect John Loughborough Pearson for modifications to the interior. Pearson was in his mid-seventies and engaged on the completion of the crowning project of his career in church architecture, the Gothic Revival Truro Cathedral. He was not really a country house man, but Astor had clearly had him on very strong recommendation

(it is not known from whom) and he reluctantly agreed to undertake both the Cliveden work and the construction of his new offices in London.[5] In fact both tasks, and the conversion of Leoni's Octagon Temple to form a family chapel, were substantially carried out by his pupil and son, Frank Loughborough Pearson. Astor's intention was to impart a more antique flavour to the rooms on the north side, as a setting for his ancient sculpture, armour, musical instruments and Renaissance works of art. The rooms on the garden side (and all the bedrooms) were redecorated by the Parisian firm of Allard, apart from the Duchess of Sutherland's 'boudoir' in the south-east corner of the ground floor, which was preserved 'as a specimen'.

The Pearsons' work at Cliveden was thus somewhat constrained; they enjoyed a far freer hand in the office and residence at 2 Temple Place on Victoria Embankment, known as Astor House and completed in 1895, a small masterpiece of romantic historicism, with an open-roofed great hall, stained glass by Clayton & Bell and woodcarvings by Thomas Nicholls. Here the staircase newels were carved by Nicholls with characters from Dumas' *Three Musketeers* in much the same fashion as W. S. Frith's historical figures at Cliveden.[6] In the decorations at Cliveden, as at the Estate Office and Astor's London house, No.18 Carlton House Terrace, the Pearsons' collaborator was J. D. Crace, who designed a new ornamental surround to Hervieu's staircase ceiling.[7]

Astor's most inspired addition to the garden was undoubtedly the balustrade from the Villa Borghese (see p.80), which he seems to have bought privately after the sale of the villa in 1892, and managed to import in 1896. At first the Italian government issued an action against the Borghese family to prevent its removal, but the Corte di Cassazione decided that it was neither a Work of Art nor an

Antiquity and therefore not subject to any regulations. These rules did prevent the removal of the statues that stood on the carved pedestals, and Astor had to find substitutes (see catalogue nos 27, 28).

If Cliveden provided Astor with an English version of the Italian villa, the purchase in 1903 of Hever Castle in Kent, the ancient home of the Boleyn family that had provided Henry VIII with his second wife, completed his investment in Old England. Here he launched Frank Pearson on the

(Left) The Annunciation and Temptation of Eve, from the mosaic decoration commissioned by the Astors for the Octagon Temple

(Right) The figures of the Duke of Buckingham and his mistress, the Countess of Shrewsbury, were carved by W. S. Frith for the Cliveden staircase, as part of the 1st Viscount Astor's remodelling of the interior

addition to the moated medieval castle of an entire 'Tudor village', and in the gardens installed a further part of his collection of antique sculpture. Astor moved to Hever after 1906 when he presented Cliveden and its collections to his son and daughter-in-law as a wedding present.

Waldorf Astor was born in 1879, and left the United States for Europe with his parents as a small boy. After preparatory school in England he was sent to Eton, and went on to New College, Oxford. When he married Nancy Langhorne Shaw, daughter of Chiswell Dabney Langhorne of Danville, Virginia, in 1906, they can hardly have seemed like compatriots at all. It was not simply that they came from different sides of the North–South conflict; before their marriage, Waldorf had never been to Virginia. Nancy had first travelled to England in the wake of a disastrous and very brief first marriage (to Robert Shaw) which ended in divorce in 1903, and returned for the following two winters for the hunting season.

Moving to Cliveden, Nancy Astor set about redecorating and refurnishing the house with the energy and confidence that would later cause Bernard Shaw to describe a stay with Nancy as like spending a Sunday with a volcano. She banished most of her father-in-law's antiquities from the 'splendid gloom' of the Hall, which she likened to the inside of a cigar box, lifted the mosaic-tiled floor, and installed chintz curtains, covers, and huge arrangements of flowers. She also introduced electric lighting.

From the very private retreat of the retiring William Waldorf Astor, Cliveden very soon became the centre of the political and literary society in which the Astors began to move. The King came to dinner in 1907, re-establishing the nineteenth-century relationship between Cliveden and Windsor Castle. Soon after their marriage, the Astors purchased a London house, No. 4 St James's Square. In the second General Election of 1910 Waldorf was elected to Parliament for Plymouth. In the years before the Great War, regular guests included writers like Henry James and Rudyard Kipling, and politicians such as Arthur Balfour, Lord Curzon and Churchill. The staff establishment had to be increased from W. W. Astor's time, and consisted of twenty in the mansion, twelve in the stables and between 40 and 50 in the garden and grounds. The footmen were recruited at a minimum of six foot in height, and wore a livery of striped red and yellow waistcoats under dark brown tailcoats.

During the First World War, the tennis court and bowling alley next to Taplow Lodge on the eastern edge of the estate were lent to the Canadian Red Cross which built a military hospital that treated over 24,000 casualties. Another and larger hospital was built on the same site by the Canadians for their soldiers in the Second World War; it continued in use until the 1980s.

William Waldorf Astor had become a British citizen in 1899. In 1916, aged nearly 70, he accepted a barony, and the following year was further

(Left) Waldorf, 2nd Viscount Astor (1879–1952), photographed by Bassano in 1935

(Right) Nancy Astor (1879–1964); by J. S. Sargent, 1908 (Hall)

ennobled with the title of Viscount. When he died in 1919, this meant that Waldorf had to break off his already successful career in the Commons and take a seat in the Lords as 2nd Viscount Astor. His unreliable health had kept him from many of the areas of public life for which he was otherwise well qualified, and there is no doubt that his enforced elevation was as great a personal blow as the loss of his father.

Within a week of the 1st Viscount's sudden death it was announced that the candidate to stand in his son's place at the ensuing by-election would be his wife Nancy. In the course of a most difficult campaign which had opened with headlines such as 'Peer's Wife Enters To Fight Against Workers At Plymouth', she first showed the spontaneous and

Nancy Astor with Bernard Shaw on the Upper Terrace at Cliveden (collection Viscount Astor)

pugnacious abilities of a natural politician, which were to make her one of the more memorable parliamentarians of the century; whether in the farcical difficulties over parliamentary protocol when she first took her seat – the first woman ever to do so[8] – or years later when she barracked Winston Churchill at the height of the Munich Crisis of 1938.

Throughout his wife's tenure of the Plymouth seat in the Commons Lord Astor took a close interest in the affairs of the city (where they had a house), serving as coalition Lord Mayor throughout the war and carrying through its controversial redevelopment plan after the blitz. At Cliveden he developed his interest in the breeding of racehorses (establishing a stud on the Taplow road) and tuberculin-free cattle at White Place Farm. His horses were highly successful, winning eleven classics, but never the Derby (five of them were placed second). He was also interested in conservation, and in the 1920s had his land on both sides of Cliveden Reach declared a Private Open Space under the Housing and Town Planning Act. He persuaded his neighbour Lord Desborough to include the Taplow Court woods in the scheme, thus ensuring the protection of the famous views from Cliveden from building development.

Between the wars the entertaining continued at Cliveden. Among the Astors' closest friends were Philip Kerr, later 11th Marquess of Lothian (who was to give his family's house at Blickling in Norfolk to the National Trust in 1942), and also celebrities such as George Bernard Shaw, with whom they visited Russia in 1931. As her son David has recalled, Lady Astor 'easily ... made contact with anybody, high or low; she was very informal and very direct, rather cheeky, and audacious in her conversation.' When Charlie Chaplin arrived for a stay in England, she telephoned to invite him to Cliveden, though they had never met, and he became a frequent visitor. At the end of Joseph Kennedy's term as US Ambassador to London in 1937, she persuaded the King to dine at Cliveden to bid him farewell. At the busiest times, particularly during Ascot week, there would always be up to 20 guests, and Harold Nicolson was probably speaking for many of them when he wrote after a visit in

The 3rd Viscount Astor replanted many of Cliveden's great beechwoods. This view south towards the Duke's Seat shows them before the storm of 1987

1936: 'There is a ghastly unreality about it all ... I enjoy seeing it. But to own it, to live here, would be like living on the stage of the Scala theatre in Milan.'[9] To Lady Astor's son Michael it was more like living in an hotel. In these years, almost for the first time, the estate took on its own, parallel social life, based on a 'club' attached to the Red Cross Hospital, with cricket matches, estate dances, and all the traditional activities that developed in the orbit of a great country house.

In the late 1930s the house parties at Cliveden began to be seen as having a more serious agenda, with the appearance of newspaper articles describing the so-called 'Cliveden Set' as the intellectual centre of Appeasement towards Hitler. The Astors had entertained the German Ambassador, Ribbentrop, at Cliveden. They were fervent supporters of Chamberlain in Parliament, and disapproved equally strongly of Churchill. But the notion of Cliveden as the setting for pro-Fascist conspiracy was wide of the mark: you were just as likely to meet the most extreme among aristocratic reactionaries as the far-left-wing MP Ellen Wilkinson or the Nazi-hater Charlie Chaplin. Depending on which list of guests he advanced, he 'could prove that Cliveden is a nest of Bolshevism, or indeed of any other bee in the world's bonnet'.[10]

The comedienne Joyce Grenfell was Nancy Astor's niece and during her childhood always went to Cliveden for Christmas, slightly in trepidation of her fierce aunt:

In the front hall we saw the giant Christmas tree was

where we expected it to be, at the foot of the oak staircase. The banisters were festooned with garlands of box, yew, bay, ivy, holly and other evergreens that, as well the humea, gave off a subtle aromatic scent … Aunt Nancy, wearing a sweater over a silk shirt, neat tweed skirt, golf socks and ghillie shoes, came out of her boudoir to greet us.

'You children go on upstairs – and take your coats with you. I will not have them left all over the place.'[11]

Lord and Lady Astor's rooms were on the first floor, and their five children occupied the 'nursery landing' on the top floor. From 1936 Joyce Grenfell lived in a cottage on the estate and during part of the war worked in the Canadian Red Cross Hospital. She entertained the troops with her revue sketches and organised concerts by Myra Hess.

It was during the Second World War that Lord Astor decided to present Cliveden to the National Trust with an endowment and many of its historic collections, expressing the hope that it might be used for the furtherance of co-operation between the peoples of Britain and North America. He lived until 1952, when he was succeeded by his son William Waldorf as 3rd Viscount, during whose time the great beechwoods were substantially re-stocked and the Rose Garden added to the grounds. The family continued to live at Cliveden until his death in 1966. His mother, Lady Astor, had died two years earlier at Grimsthorpe in Lincolnshire, the home of her daughter Nancy, Countess of Ancaster.

In July 1961 it was at Cliveden, where he had rented a cottage for some years, that the osteopath Stephen Ward first introduced the Secretary of State for War John Profumo to Christine Keeler. The revelation in 1963 of her acquaintance with the Soviet GRU officer Captain Ivanov, and the War Secretary's denial of any 'impropriety', ended Profumo's political career and gravely weakened the Macmillan government. While these events, of a summer weekend at the end of almost 300 not uneventful years, became the stuff of newspaper headlines, by the standards of the 2nd Duke of Buckingham, they did not amount to very much.

In 1966 the house was let to Stanford University of California as the centre for their English educational programmes, in accordance with the 2nd Lord Astor's wishes. In 1984–5, at the end of the University's lease, the National Trust undertook major repairs to the fabric of the house, reroofing it and repairing the façades and terracotta ornaments. Meanwhile, Cliveden Hotel Ltd took a 100-year lease of the house and carried out the thorough restoration, conversion and redecoration of the interior.

The lease to the hotel ensures the maintenance of a high standard of presentation, provides a rental income for the Trust's management of the estate, and allows public access. It also perpetuates the traditional use of Cliveden as a place of resort and entertainment.

In the 1990s the Trust is continuing the capital repair of other major parts of the property, including the clock-tower, terrace and balustrades, with the support of grant-aid from English Heritage.

NOTES

1 Quoted from the American press of c.1899 in Michael Astor, *Tribal Feeling*, 1963, p.16.

2 Ibid.

3 In 1910, W. W. Astor and his son Waldorf bought the *Observer*, in later years edited by Waldorf's son David. W. W. Astor's younger son, John Jacob Astor V, 1st Lord Astor of Hever, owned *The Times* from 1922 to 1966.

4 Oral reminiscence of Mrs Emily Lee, 1993.

5 Anthony Quiney, *John Loughborough Pearson*, 1979, pp.218–20.

6 Astor House was sold after the 1st Viscount's death in 1919 and it was probably at that time that the chimney-piece carved with the Astor pedigree was brought to Cliveden and set up in the Sounding Room. The office was damaged by a flying bomb in 1944 but well restored.

7 Megan Aldrich, ed., *The Craces*, 1990, pp.128–32.

8 The first woman *elected* was Constance Gore-Booth, Countess Markiewicz, for a Dublin constituency in December 1918, in the Sinn Fein interest. She refused the oath of allegiance and never assumed her seat. Nancy Astor remained the solitary female MP until the election of Mrs Wintringham for the Liberals in 1921.

9 *Diary*, 28 June 1936.

10 Quoted in Sykes, 1972, p.401.

11 Joyce Grenfell, *In Pleasant Places*, 1980, p.191.

FAMILY TREE OF THE ASTORS

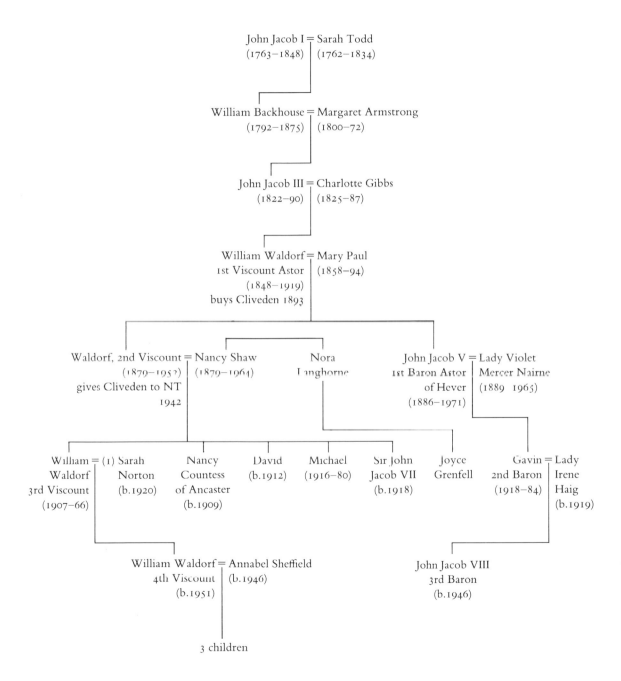

John Jacob I = Sarah Todd
(1763–1848) | (1762–1834)

William Backhouse = Margaret Armstrong
(1792–1875) | (1800–72)

John Jacob III = Charlotte Gibbs
(1822–90) | (1825–87)

William Waldorf = Mary Paul
1st Viscount Astor | (1858–94)
(1848–1919)
buys Cliveden 1893

Waldorf, 2nd Viscount = Nancy Shaw
(1879–1952) | (1879–1964)
gives Cliveden to NT
1942

Nora
Langhorne

John Jacob V = Lady Violet
1st Baron Astor | Mercer Nairne
of Hever | (1889–1965)
(1886–1971)

William = (1) Sarah
Waldorf | Norton
3rd Viscount | (b.1920)
(1907–66)

Nancy
Countess
of Ancaster
(b.1909)

David
(b.1912)

Michael
(1916–80)

Sir John
Jacob VII
(b.1918)

Joyce
Grenfell

Gavin = Lady
2nd Baron | Irene
(1918–84) | Haig
(b.1919)

William Waldorf = Annabel Sheffield
4th Viscount | (b.1946)
(b.1951)

John Jacob VIII
3rd Baron
(b.1946)

3 children

CHAPTER FIVE
THE GARDEN AND GROUNDS

Cliveden was laid out as a formal garden during the first half of the eighteenth century. But for a garden as large and long established, it is disappointing that first-hand documentary evidence about its history is so sparse.[1] And what does exist is tantalising, for it deals in the main with proposals which were never carried out. Any account of its development must, therefore, necessarily be largely a matter of deduction. Three owners have played a major role in the making of the garden as we know it today: the 1st Lord Orkney, the 2nd Duke and Duchess of Sutherland, and the Astor family. Owners subsequent to Lord Orkney have tended to build on the work of their predecessors, so the garden is like a palimpsest with one scheme laid on, but not obliterating, a previous scheme, and Lord Orkney's firm imprint is still discernible.

The chalk cliffs described by Leland in 1538 had probably altered little when, in the late 1660s, on the highest part of this ground, the 2nd Duke of Buckingham commissioned William Winde to erect the first of the three houses to occupy the present site. To provide a flat space on which to build, the hill was levelled and a long terrace built above a blind arcade. Nothing is known of the garden the Duke must have made on this newly levelled ground. Evelyn, who visited Cliveden in 1679, mentioned gardens and an avenue through the woods, but wrote disapprovingly of 'the land about all barren and producing nothing but ferne'.[2]

The 1st Earl of Orkney, who bought Cliveden in 1696, was engaged from at least 1706 until the year of his death in 1737 in laying out the garden. He turned his attention first to proposals for the ground below the terrace; in January 1706 he wrote to tell his brother that 'as for the ground behind the house I have a plan how I should turn it' but, he added, 'I see no manner of Esperaunce of my doing it as yet'.[3] The plan then being considered may possibly be a

drawing which on style has been attributed to Henry Wise, master-gardener to Queen Anne, for whom he laid out the grounds of Hampton Court and Kensington Palace. Another letter of the following month reported '20 or 30 men att work ... and planting and other things doeing' but shortage of funds seems to have prevented Lord Orkney from undertaking all he wished to do at this time. By April 1707 he had had to decide that 'as for either altering these gardens before the house or macking new behind I give over thought of both at present'.

In the following decade, when he again considered proposals for this ground behind the house, Lord Orkney, in spite of a military career fighting the French, turned to France for advice. Claude Desgots, Le Nôtre's nephew and successor as chief garden designer to Louis XIV, sent him two parterre designs, each inscribed on the back 'à Versailles le Juillet 1713', together with a memorandum explaining some further designs which no longer exist. In his memorandum, Desgots also gave advice on the levelling of the ground, on the planting of trees and shrubs such as honeysuckle, Persian lilac and jasmine and counselled that an intelligent man would be needed to make the garden and place the soil. Interestingly, even as early as this, he said he would make no mention of the grass because he was convinced there was nowhere in the world that it was so beautifully and so well looked after as in England.

Lord Orkney's main intention at the time seems to have been the enlarging of the Parterre, which was probably a good deal shorter than it is now. A group of three further designs, of which that illustrated on p.51 is the most elaborate, suggests alternative treatments and shows the site more accurately by means of a related drawing. None of these drawings is signed or dated, but they can be presumed to have been prepared shortly after

Desgots' and possibly by the 'intelligent man' he recommended. The high quality of their draughts-manship and obvious influence of the Le Nôtre school suggests a French designer working in this country. A parallel has been drawn between the crisply shaped mound at the southern end of the Parterre and the ziggurat of similar shape in a drawing by a surveyor called Bourguignon for Lord Petre's garden at Thorndon Hall in Essex.[4]

After all these ambitious schemes, Lord Orkney settled on a far simpler solution during the winter of

Design for a parterre, probably for Cliveden, and believed to be by Henry Wise (collection Viscount Astor)

1723–4. In a letter to his brother on 5 December, he reported that he had been:

this fortnight at Cliefden struling with wind and rain to get new trees planted ... and the trees looks like soe many stickes and will doe soe for some years yet I bleive you will not dislike it I call it a Quaker parter for it is very plain and yet I beleeve you will think it noble.

His solution was a plain rectangular grass sward (in place of *broderie* beds) with raised walks on either side and a circular depression at the far end, bordered all round with a double row of elm trees. And it appears thus in a drawing by an anonymous Frenchman to explain the construction and method of laying down a land drain to repair a breach in the steep hillside above the river.

A further drawing, for the river or slope immediately below the terrace, shows an elaborate arrangement of paths, steps, watercourses and, alongside a sunken enclosure shaped like a Roman circus, an amphitheatre. (In 1735, Leoni's Octagon Temple was to be built in the place of the tree within a semicircle and much later still the 1st Viscount Astor was to make an Italian Garden in place of the circus.) The drawing was almost certainly made by the same anonymous Frenchman, as its scale is measured in *pieds* and may be connected with a letter of 2 October 1723 from Lord Orkney to his brother confessing that even though his expenditure of 'sans exagère ... 13 or 14 livres a day ever since I begun ... mackes very little appearance yet ... it is a greater work than I thought ...', he still thinks ' ... it will be much better than was intended'. The letter is also interesting because it reveals that Lord Orkney called on the help of an English garden designer as well. It continues:

... besides ther is great difficulty to get the slope all that side of the Hill where the precipice was, but Bridge-man mackes difficultys of nothing I told him if I thought to had been the one Half of what I see it will cost I believe I never had done it, he says the beginning is the worst ...

It seems clear that Lord Orkney and Charles Bridgeman were attempting to put into effect, with some difficulty and exasperation, the complex French formal designs already in Lord Orkney's possession, and only parts were used, either for practical or aesthetic reasons. In the event, an amphitheatre, though in much simplified form, was made at the northern end of the river slope, where it remains to this day.

As has been said, Lord Orkney's appetite for planting and gardening activities in no way diminished with advancing years. Only a year before his death he received a letter from his friend Alexander Pope, which talks of their meeting in London for '... the pleasure of planning and drawing schemes, as well as of seeing you and consulting you agst ye next planting season ...'.[5] Whether or not Pope left

his hand on any part of the garden at Cliveden is not now known.

Tradition has it that Frederick, Prince of Wales laid out parts of the garden, in particular the area now known as the Ilex Grove. But the Prince's surviving account books include no sums of extra-ordinary garden expenditure, except regular payments to John Morris, the head gardener. Indeed, under an agreement Morris made with the Prince in 1737, he undertook to maintain the gardens 'as well as they were at any time kept during the time when the late Earl of Orkney used and enjoyed the same'.[6]

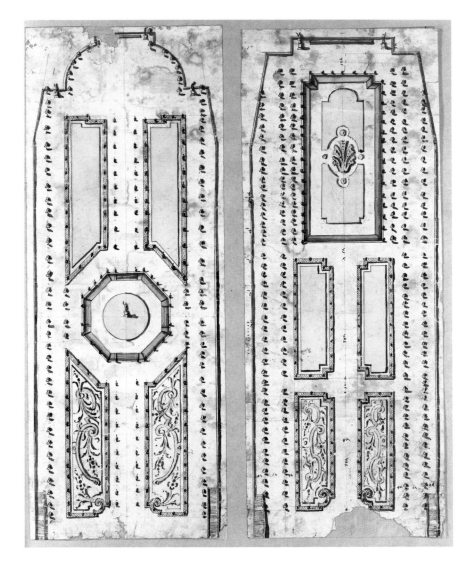

(Left) Designs for parterres by Claude Desgots, 1713 (collection Viscount Astor)

(Right) Early eighteenth-century design for a parterre, probably by a French draughtsman (collection Viscount Astor)

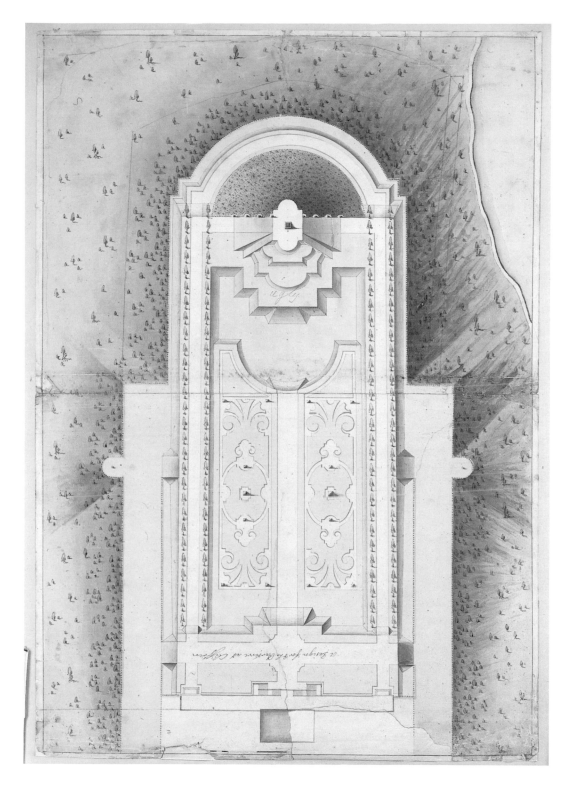

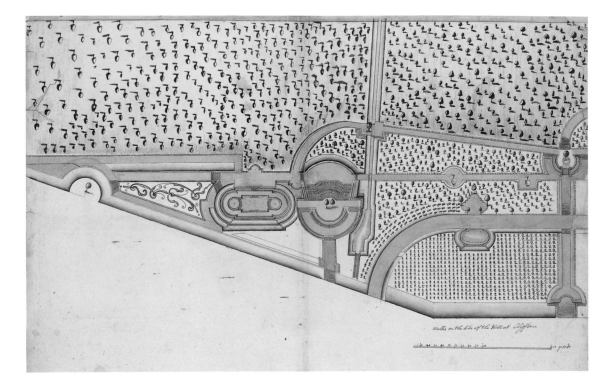

(Above) 'Walks on the Side of the Hill at Cliffden', a design of c.1723 for the lower part of the garden (collection Viscount Astor)

(Right) 'A Plan of the Upper part of Clifden Gardens', in the style of Charles Bridgeman (collection Viscount Astor)

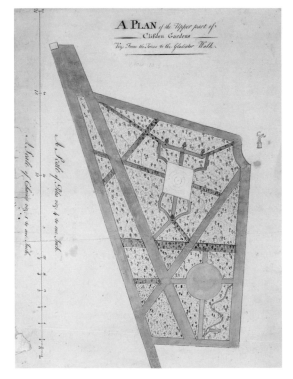

Moreover, the pattern of the Ilex Grove in a drawing close in style and lettering to Bridgeman's other known work differs little from that in surveys of 1749 by John Richardson (made during the Prince's tenancy) and of 1762 by Samuel Andrews.[7] It has the same two avenues which meet at their apex at the Blenheim Pavilion, is enclosed by avenues on the north (the present Queen's Walk) and on the west (Grand Avenue) and has the same circular enclosure (now occupied by the Rose Garden).

Andrews's survey was made during the ownership of Mary, Countess of Orkney (who inherited Cliveden from her mother Anne in 1756) and is likely to represent the garden layout very much as Lord Orkney left it. In place then were the 'Quaker'

The Parterre in the late nineteenth century, with the
wedge-shaped beds planted by John Fleming

parterre, the Yew Tree Walk (leading from the Octagon Temple to the river), and the wooded river slope to the north of the Temple 'cutt out very agreeably in walks and *vistos* yt present the most beautiful prospects of ye river'.[8] The Grand Avenue then continued across the road in the form of a double avenue, and the road itself was bordered by an avenue culminating in a *rond-point*, from which sprang radiating avenues. Green Drive then formed the boundary with Taplow Common. Across the present Russian Valley ran three avenues aligned on the east front of the house; on the hill side facing the Parterre there were a shorter Grand Walk than now along the top of the river cliff and three cross avenues, one terminating at the Half Moon, another passing the present Duke's Seat and the southern-most forming the then boundary with Taplow Court.

Comparison of this survey with an engraved survey map made to accompany auction particulars in 1818 reveals that by the latter date many of the avenues had disappeared, as had most of the trees on the Parterre, and there had been a considerable loosening-up of the formal planting.

Formality, in a nineteenth-century style, was to be returned to parts of the garden during the ownership of the 2nd Duke and Duchess of Sutherland. Under the supervision of their able head gardener, John Fleming, Cliveden was to become horticulturally famous. Like Lord Orkney, the Sutherlands turned their attention first to the Parterre, then a vast waste of lawn. The Sutherlands considered a number of designs from several land-scape gardeners,[9] including one from Sir Charles Barry, but the plan they finally adopted in 1853 was made by their own head gardener, who later published and described his design.[10] On either side of a wide grass path were eight interlocking wedge-shaped beds, each with a centre bed surrounded by a raised grass border. All these beds had an edging of clipped privet and spruce. Circles were cut in the grass between each pair of beds, the outer row filled with dwarf- and half-standard roses, the inner row with bedding. The centre beds were planted with azaleas and rhododendrons alternately, with space for gladioli, foxgloves and hollyhocks in summer. The outer, belt-shaped beds were treated to left and right of the central path in pairs and in the spring of 1862, the year Fleming's drawing was published, they contained blue and white forget-me-not, pink and white Silene, mixed anemones, daisies and masses of tulips. Each bed took 2,000 plants and 800 tulips. As soon as the spring flowers were over they were replaced with half-hardy summer plants. Though their components have changed, the beds today retain the shape Fleming gave them. The circle at the far end of the Parterre has, however, an older history than the triangular beds, being part of Lord Orkney's original layout. Fleming also planted the top of its inner raised bank. Red and white lilacs and thorns to harmonise with the azaleas and rhododendrons lined the long turf banks of the level lawn.

In addition to the Parterre beds, Fleming made wavy 'ribbon' borders immediately below the terrace; no fewer than 40 pear-shaped beds in the Duke's Garden; a huge raised grass circle in the forecourt, which had in its centre a deodar cedar surrounded by the four varieties of pansy bred at Cliveden; and winding in the grass amongst the evergreen oaks of the Ilex Grove, by then already

grown to great size, a ribbon border two feet wide and upwards of 300 yards in length, with bows and knots where the space permitted.[11] All these beds were filled with a colourful but carefully blended mixture of plants. Under Fleming's direction bedding reached a level never before attained. His particular innovation was to replace the tender summer-flowering bedding by winter- and spring-flowering plants, including bulbs, rather than the evergreens or plain soil beds which had previously been the custom – a practice ever since adopted universally. In 1868 the bedding included the Duchess of Sutherland's monogram 'HS' picked out in flowers. Fleming explained his methods and the plant associations he used in his influential book *Spring and Winter Flower Gardening*, first published *c*.1864.

No less attention was lavished on the wilder parts of the garden. Fleming planted great swathes of bluebells, snowdrops, primroses, wood anemones and other wild flowers in the woods. His influence persisted throughout the 2nd Duke of Westminster's time and even after his retirement, until at least the early years of the 1st Viscount Astor's ownership.

The 1st Lord Astor added much to the garden. Besides the Borghese Balustrade he introduced much other fine statuary, as described in Chapter

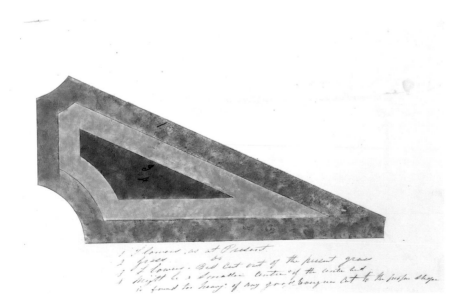

Fleming's planting plan for one of his beds on the Parterre

A topiary bird in the Long Garden, which was laid out by the 1st Lord Astor

Seven, and formed an Italian Garden near to the Octagon Temple, laid out the Long Garden, designed and planted a maze (which no longer exists) and introduced the pagoda to what is now the Water Garden. His son and daughter-in-law planted herbaceous borders in the forecourt and conceived the idea of the central open space in the Long Garden, the latter designed by Norah Lindsay, who was also commissioned by Lady Astor to dress the house for parties with lavish floral displays. Mrs Lindsay began her influential career as a garden designer at Cliveden and was later to work at Blickling for the Astors' friend Lord Lothian. Lord Astor enlarged the skating pond to a Water Garden and adapted the Italian Garden as a cemetery for those who died in the Canadian Hospital at Cliveden during the First World War. He was an enthusiastic tree planter, causing much underplanting to be done in the woods. The Lombardy poplars which punctuate the flat fields of the river plain also owe their existence to him. The 3rd Viscount Astor enriched many of the rides and woodlands with rhododendrons and planted the Rose Garden within a layout of beds and panels of gravel designed by Sir Geoffrey Jellicoe in abstract shapes taken from a painting by Paul Klee.

During the last three decades or so that the National Trust has maintained the garden, it has considerably extended the Water Garden and increased the variety of its plants, redesigned and planted the forecourt with herbaceous borders, planted the beds of the Parterre and Long Garden with perennial plants and nursed their box hedges to good health, and trimmed back innumerable laurels which had crept over the lawns throughout the drives. A lime avenue and yew walk lead down to the river, and limes frame the Parterre and the Shell Fountain. Much replanting in the woods has been done, but after the devastating storm which caused such havoc in 1990 it will be a continuing job for many years to come.

NOTES

1 The surviving eighteenth- and nineteenth-century architectural drawings, garden designs, engravings and manuscripts to do with Cliveden were bound in an album by the 1st Viscount Astor c.1905. The album, known as the Cliveden Album, is in the possession of the present Lord Astor. Most of the garden designs have been published and many illustrated in Gervase Jackson-Stops, 'Formal Garden Designs for Cliveden: The Work of Claude Desgots and Others for the 1st Earl of Orkney', *National Trust Yearbook*, 1976–7, pp.100–17.

2 Entry for 23 July 1679, *Diary of John Evelyn*, ed. de Beer, iv, 1955.

3 National Library of Scotland, MSS 1033.

4 Gervase Jackson-Stops, op. cit., n.1.

5 Northumberland Record Office. Craster Papers 'From ZCR9'.

6 Cliveden Album, p.82.

7 Both John Richardson's and Samuel Andrews's surveys are at the Buckinghamshire Record Office.

8 Extract from the *Diaries of Jeremiah Milles*, 1742. British Library Add. MSS 15776 fs.118–19.

9 *The Gardener's Chronicle*, 21 July 1877. But the names of the garden designers are not given.

10 J. Fleming, 'Bedding-out at Cliveden', *Journal of Horticulture and Cottage Gardener*, 29 July 1862, pp.336–7 and coloured supplement.

11 *Journal of Horticulture and Cottage Gardener*, 7 June 1864, pp.416–17.

CHAPTER SIX
THE SCULPTURE

The long history of the house, garden and grounds at Cliveden has led to the concentration here of extensive and important sculpture collections. Above all, these testify to the contrasting tastes of the 2nd Duke and Duchess of Sutherland and William Waldorf, 1st Viscount Astor. The collection can be divided into two groups: the garden sculpture, scattered throughout the extensive parterres, groves and slopes of the grounds, and inside the house, the sculpted portrait and genre busts, and the grand carved stone fireplace with its bronze firedogs.

The 2nd Duke and Duchess of Sutherland appear to have been the first proprietors of Cliveden to have collected sculpture for display in the grounds, and we know that the Duchess of Sutherland's earlier collaboration with Sir Charles Barry at Trentham had engendered an interest in arranging sculpture in the open. Although Lord Astor made further extensive changes to the grounds and to the interior of the house, he incorporated much of the garden sculpture left by the Sutherlands into his schemes. Evidently neither the 3rd Duke of Sutherland, nor his brother-in-law, the Duke of Westminster, showed much interest in the sculpture collection, for they were sold to Lord Astor together with the house. Even the statue most closely associated with the Sutherlands, Matthew Noble's colossal full-length portrait of *The 2nd Duke of Sutherland* (*31**; 1866; a bronze copy is at Dunrobin Castle), was included in the sale, although it was removed in 1896 by Lord Astor from its former prominent site at the head of the Grand Avenue to the Duke's Seat in a more remote position in the woods.[1] Some of the indoor sculpture was removed after the sale of the house and distributed among the family, but apparently nothing from the garden. The documentary evidence does not, however, allow us firmly to associate every statue with one or other of these collectors, and in such instances a certain amount of guesswork is required, based on what we know of their personal tastes and collecting habits.

The Sutherlands had close ties with the British and French royal families, and many of their choices appear to have been influenced by these contacts.[2] The sculpture most closely associated with the Sutherlands, and reflecting their royal friendships, are mainly gathered in the Ilex Grove. These include William Theed the Younger's electrotype cast of *Prince Albert* (*30*; 1865), given to the Duchess by Queen Victoria after the Prince Consort's death, in commemoration of their long-standing friendship and the Duchess's 'very great and sincere admiration of the Prince . . .',[3] and the bronze *Joan of Arc* (*29*; *c.*1838), by Princesse Marie-Christine d'Orléans, probably a gift from the French king, Louis-Philippe, in memory of the princess after her untimely death in 1839.[4] In his life of St Joan, Ronald Gower recorded that his mother, the Duchess, 'had what the French call a "culte" for the heroine'.[5]

The Sutherlands' taste for French contemporary sculpture was largely formed during their years of travel in France in the 1830s. It was also influenced by acquaintances who, in addition to the royal family, included the prominent collector James de Rothschild, an important patron of the bronze sculptor Jean-Jacques Feuchère, who was to be commissioned to execute portraits of their son, the *Marquess of Stafford* (1837; now at Dunrobin Castle), and of Adolphe Thiers, the French Minister of the Interior and former art critic.[6] In the 1850s they also commissioned the French sculptor A.-E. Carrier-Belleuse to portray their two younger sons *Lord Ronald Leveson-Gower* and *Lord Albert Leveson-Gower* (bronze statuettes, 1852; Dunrobin Castle,

* See Catalogue of Garden Sculpture, p.78.

formerly at Cliveden), again in fancifully historic costume. During that period Carrier-Belleuse was employed to produce sculptural models for the Minton ceramics factory in Staffordshire, perhaps brought there through the Duchess, who took a personal interest in the factory.[7] The Duchess was also one of the earliest patrons of the Scottish sculptor Alexander Munro, who carved the reliefs in Caen stone of *The Four Seasons* (1853; Terrace). These were originally intended to ornament a fireplace similar to the one he had carved for Dunrobin in 1847–8. He also carved a marble

portrait of the Duchess's daughter, *Lady Grosvenor* (1852–3; formerly at Cliveden

Elsewhere in the gardens at Cliveden, e the Sutherlands' fondness for nineteenth-century Neo-classical sculpture is illustrated by Thorvaldsen's marble *Mercury about to kill Argus* (21) in the Ilex Grove, and Rinaldi's *Delphic Sibyl* (22), situated below the Amphitheatre. The *Mercury* is rare among Thorvaldsen's works in being based on a real figure, the pose apparently suggested by the sight of a young man on the roadside, whom he drew in a series of rapid sketches.

(31) The 2nd Duke of Sutherland; by Matthew Noble, 1866 (Duke's Seat)

Lord Astor's tastes had been formed over several years' travel in Europe, and his choices are typical of those we might expect of a highly cultured late nineteenth-century transatlantic collector and connoisseur. In Italy he had taken the opportunity of acquiring an impressive collection of Classical Roman sarcophagi and other Classical sculpture from the Borghese collection, as well as from several other prominent Roman and Florentine collections, and through private dealers. The precise sources of Lord Astor's acquisitions are often vague, although we know that he bought through the renowned Florentine dealer Stefano Bardini,[9] and through the Roman dealers Sangiorgi and Simonetti. In London, he bought from Partridge, Mallet and Trollope. With the exception of sculpture bought at public auction, our only further information derives from a set of typewritten notes made in 1920 (based on notes which were probably compiled around 1905, and amplified by the 2nd Lord

(Left) (21) Mercury about to kill Argus; by Bertel Thorvaldsen (Ilex Grove)

(Far right) (32) The Wounded Amazon; by William Waldorf Astor (Rose Garden)

Astor in 1944).[10] Regrettably, they give only general indications of where and when Lord Astor bought items for his collection.

The substantial collection of Classical Roman sculpture is divided between the gardens of Cliveden and Astor's other country residence at Hever Castle in Kent, where there are still over 100 pieces, including a further sixteen sarcophagi. Even after his death in 1919, further Classical sculpture was brought to England from his villa in Sorrento, some of which was placed in the Rose Garden. The sculptures include versions of the *Venus d'Este* (*25*) and the *Satyr resting* (*26*), as well as William Waldorf Astor's own youthful attempt at sculpture, his *Wounded Amazon* (*32*), dated 1870, and perhaps carved under the direction of William Wetmore Story (1819–95), the American dilettante sculptor based in Rome, whose most renowned work, *Cleopatra* (1858), was immortalised in Nathaniel Hawthorne's book *The Marble Faun* (1860).[11] Story's studio in the Palazzo Barberini in Rome, where he had settled in 1856, was the centre of American expatriate cultural life, and included Hawthorne and Henry James among its *habitués*, and no doubt Astor frequented its gatherings while he was resident in Italy.

Lord Astor also acquired post-Classical sculptures from the Gatterburg-Morosini sale in Venice in 1894, and in France he bought from two important sales: the Spitzer collection (1892) and Lord Hertford's collection at Bagatelle in Paris (1900). He also bought several interesting contemporary works, mainly by Italian sculptors and foreign sculptors resident in Italy. Among these is the colossal *Fountain of Love* (*33*), situated in the Grand Avenue, designed and carved in Rome by Thomas Waldo Story (1855–1915), the son and pupil of William Wetmore Story. It is signed and dated 'Waldo Story Roma 1897'. Story was also employed to make a copy of the Borghese Balustrade (see below) for the steps leading up from the landing stage, and a bronze figure of the *Duke of Marlborough*, which once stood in the Blenheim Pavilion situated to the north of the house. Story's work was popular in the circles in which Astor moved; for British and American clients he produced portrait busts, monuments and decorative sculpture, including a

fountain in the park at Blenheim for the Duke of Marlborough (whose wife, the American heiress Consuelo Vanderbilt, knew Story from Rome). At Ascott in Buckinghamshire he created a marble and bronze fountain of the *Triumph of Galatea* for Leopold de Rothschild, and decorative sculpture for Lord Rothschild's billiard-room at Tring Park, Buckinghamshire.[12]

Astor's importance as a collector depends not only on these acquisitions, which conform to the

contemporary notion of acceptable good taste at the end of the nineteenth century, but on a group of works of exceptional quality and importance in the history of sculpture. These include the Borghese Balustrade (17) and the bronze group of the *Rape of Proserpina* (16), attributed to the Florentine sculptor Vincenzo de' Rossi (1525–87),[13] both acquired around 1896 from the Borghese collection in Rome, and the pair of French eighteenth-century marble *Handmaidens of Diana* (27, 28) by Claude-Auguste Cayot (1677–1722) and Claude Poirier (1656–1729), bought from Bagatelle and originally destined for Louis XlV's park at Marly.[14] Astor initially placed these on the pedestals at the end of the balustrade, in imitation of the Classical statues that had originally stood on the balustrade while it remained at the Villa Borghese. (They have been removed for conservation.)

W. W. Astor's collecting of Italian sculpture co-incided with the introduction of the first mains water supply to Venice. The Verona marble or Istrian stone well-heads that had ornamented hundreds of public and private wells became redundant and available to collectors. Those at Cliveden are complemented by a further nine examples at Hever. They date variously from the fifteenth to the sixteenth centuries.

After Lord Astor's death further changes were made by his son, the 2nd Lord Astor: the War Memorial Garden was adapted from the existing Italian Garden in 1918, and the bronze statue of a *Female figure* (35) – a portrait of Nancy Astor – by the Australian sculptor Sir Bertram MacKennal (1863–1931) was placed there.[15] Later on, the 3rd Lord Astor rearranged the Rose Garden, installing Classical sculpture, as noted above.

The sculpture collection at Cliveden is wide-ranging in its coverage of styles and types of

(33) The Fountain of Love; by Thomas Waldo Story

(16) The Rape of Proserpina; attributed to Vincenzo de' Rossi (Parterre). The original is now in the Victoria and Albert Museum

sculpture – inevitably, given its complicated history. Yet it is possible to identify two patterns of collecting: Lord Astor's predilection for the Classical past is represented by the collection of Roman sarcophagi and Classical originals, or copies after antique masterpieces, which provide the foil for his eclectic acquisitions of post-Classical sculpture. The Sutherlands' taste followed a more easily classifiable course: the bias was mainly towards contemporary French and British sculpture with the occasional *de rigueur* Neo-classical statue acquired by the Duke on his Grand Tour. Combined, these collections form a remarkably eclectic and well-preserved open-air sculpture gallery.

NOTES

1 According to a list dated 1868 among the Sutherland Papers in Staffordshire Record Office, the family had intended to remove it to Trentham. Noble also produced a portrait of the Duke for the North Staffordshire Waterworks Company, and designed the memorials to the Duchess at Trentham (1868) and Dunrobin (1869).

2 See Philip Ward-Jackson, 'A.-E. Carrier-Belleuse, J.-J. Feuchère and the Sutherlands', *Burlington Magazine*, cxxvii, 1985, p.147ff., for a detailed study of the Sutherlands' patronage of French sculptors and their connections with the French royal family.

3 Theodore Martin, *The Life of His Royal Highness*, London, 1876, ii, p.245, n.3. According to four drawings by Clutton in the Cliveden Album, the statue was at one stage to be placed on the east face of the clock-tower.

4 Ward-Jackson, op. cit., p.147, n.1.

5 Lord Ronald Gower, *Joan of Arc*, London, 1893.

6 Ward-Jackson, op. cit., pp.147–8.

7 Ibid., p.150.

8 B. Read and J. Barnes, ed., *Pre-Raphaelite Sculpture*, London, 1992, p.112.

9 See Gavin Astor, *Statuary and Sculpture at Hever*, Ipswich, 1969, p.8, no 74, where he states that a sarcophagus at Hever Castle was 'last recorded in the hands of a dealer, Bardini, in Florence'.

10 These notes are now preserved at the National Trust Regional Office at Hughenden Manor, Buckinghamshire.

11 See Henry James, *William Wetmore Story and his Friends*, 2 vols, Boston, 1903. For biography and further bibliography, see *Two Hundred Years of American Sculpture* (exh. cat.), Whitney Museum of American Art, New York, 1976, p.314, and *American Artists in Europe* (exh. cat.), Walker Art Gallery, Liverpool, 1976–7.

12 See E. M. Philip, *Magazine of Art*, 1903, pp.137–41, 375ff., and *American Art News*, xiv, 1914/15, no.4, p.5.

13 See A. Boström, 'A Rediscovered Florentine Bronze Group of the Rape of Proserpina at Cliveden', *Burlington Magazine*, cxxxii, December 1990, pp.828–40.

14 See Terence Hodgkinson, 'Companions of Diana at Cliveden', *National Trust Studies*, 1979, pp.91–8.

15 See M. H. Spielmann, *British Sculpture and Sculptors of Today*, 1901, p.132; and *British Sculpture, 1850–1914* (exh. cat.), The Fine Art Society, 1968, p.28, nos 106–9, see also G. Sturgeon, *The Development of Australian Sculpture 1788–1975*, London, 1978, pp.57–70.

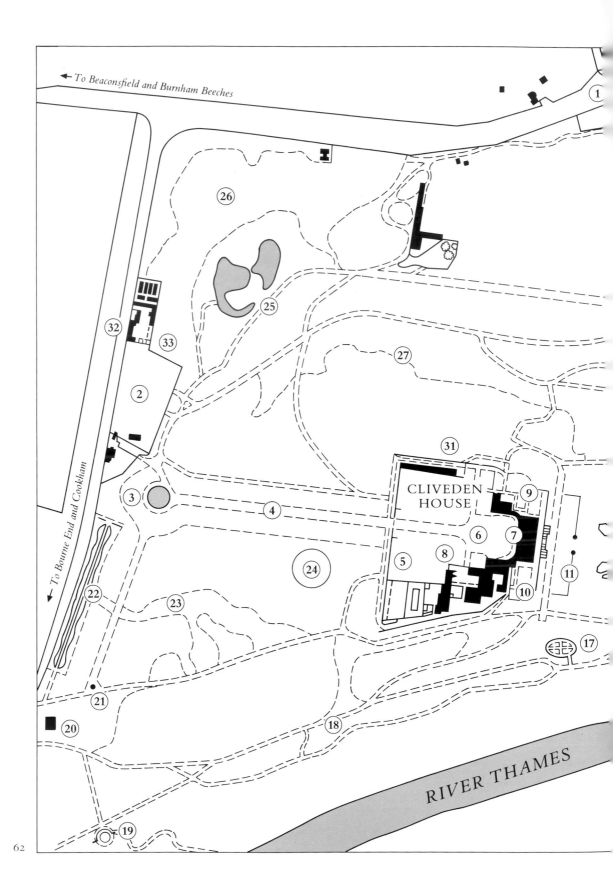

To Beaconsfield and Burnham Beeches

CLIVEDEN HOUSE

RIVER THAMES

To Bourne End and Cookham

62

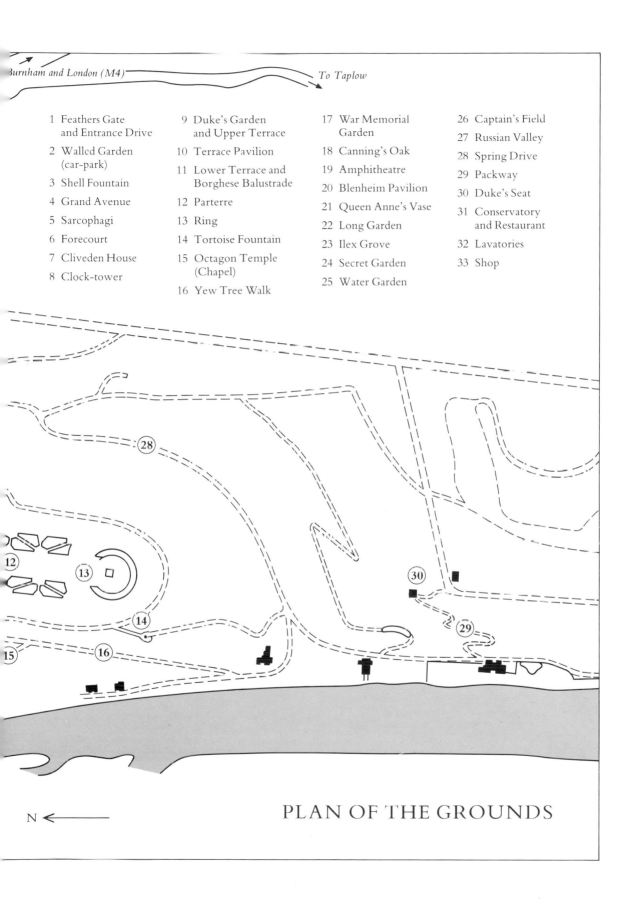

To Burnham and London (M4) ———— To Taplow

1 Feathers Gate and Entrance Drive
2 Walled Garden (car-park)
3 Shell Fountain
4 Grand Avenue
5 Sarcophagi
6 Forecourt
7 Cliveden House
8 Clock-tower

9 Duke's Garden and Upper Terrace
10 Terrace Pavilion
11 Lower Terrace and Borghese Balustrade
12 Parterre
13 Ring
14 Tortoise Fountain
15 Octagon Temple (Chapel)
16 Yew Tree Walk

17 War Memorial Garden
18 Canning's Oak
19 Amphitheatre
20 Blenheim Pavilion
21 Queen Anne's Vase
22 Long Garden
23 Ilex Grove
24 Secret Garden
25 Water Garden

26 Captain's Field
27 Russian Valley
28 Spring Drive
29 Packway
30 Duke's Seat
31 Conservatory and Restaurant
32 Lavatories
33 Shop

N ←

PLAN OF THE GROUNDS

CHAPTER SEVEN
TOUR OF THE GARDEN AND GROUNDS

Numbers in brackets refer to the key of the plan of Cliveden, reproduced on p.62. The main features of interest are described here in the same order as listed in the key, providing visitors with a suggested itinerary. A catalogue of the principal garden statuary is given on p.78, and numbers in italic type refer to this list.

THE FEATHERS GATE AND ENTRANCE DRIVE (1)

The present, serpentine approach to the house from the Feathers Gate on the Taplow road has only been the principal entrance for about a hundred years. Until then the house had always been approached by the main northern axis drive. The Feathers Gate takes its name from the inn opposite, formerly the Three Feathers (in honour of Frederick, Prince of Wales, who leased Cliveden from 1739 to 1751).

The elaborate wrought-iron gates bearing the monogram of W. W. Astor were made in 1893 by the firm of Singer of Frome. They were repaired between 1979 and 1981 with the support of a grant from the Ironmongers' Company. The adjacent lodge was added in 1901.

THE WALLED GARDEN (2)

Visitors park in what was formerly a walled garden, disbanded after the Second World War. The marks and whitewash around the walls were left by glasshouses or by the 'wall-glazing' pioneered by John Fleming, head gardener to the Sutherlands from the 1850s, but the principal 'glass department' was in another, older-established walled enclosure to the north-west of the house. In 1877 this had five glasshouses for vines, three for peaches and nectarines, and one each for melons, apricots, figs and

(Right) Cliveden from the north-east

(Left) One of the herbaceous borders that flank the forecourt lawns

cucumbers, with others devoted to ferns and other plants for the house, including gardenias, stephanotis and orchids.

In the yard beyond the Walled Garden, gas was produced for consumption on the estate. The chimney of the retort house was clad in cement modelled to resemble a tree trunk.

THE SHELL FOUNTAIN (3)
AND GRAND AVENUE (4)

From the car-park, the drive continues towards a *rond-point* at the end of the north axis of the house, which was probably first laid out around 1706 by Lord Orkney. The avenue of tall limes, 460 yards long and aligned on the inner faces of the two wings of the house, formerly stretched as far again to the north, beyond the main gate to the Hedsor road.

This was known as the 'Gladiator's Gate' after a statue of the Borghese Gladiator that stood at the centre of the *rond-point*. Thomas Waldo Story's *Fountain of Love* (35), now in its place, was set up here in 1897. The inner avenue of lime trees was planted in 1997 to replace the long-lost originals.

THE FORECOURT (6)
AND CLOCK-TOWER (8)

An engraving of the north front of Cliveden in 1752 (illustrated on p.14) shows the great yew hedge flanking the entrance to the courtyard already about eight feet high. The four piers at the entrance, and the ironwork between them, were designed for the Duke (then Marquess) of Westminster in 1869 by Henry Clutton, who added the *porte-cochère*, the stables with their courtyard and screens, and the

The south front

loggias either side of the clock-tower, at the same time. The tower itself had been built by Clutton eight years earlier (1861) for the Duke's mother-in-law, the Duchess of Sutherland. Among its 'mixed and lushly transmogrified sources' (Pevsner) are blended Italian and French Renaissance motifs: the half-open spiral staircase recalls that at Blois. At its top there is, as there was on top of Barry's earlier tower at Trentham (on which this is based), a version of Augustin Dumont's *Le Génie de la Liberté* (*Spirit of Liberty*) made for the July Column in the Place de la Bastille, Paris. The cast-bronze surrounds to the clock faces, the bronze urns on the balconies and the carved keystone and stone urns on the loggia are embellishments of the 1st Lord Astor, most probably by Waldo Story. The original scheme of gilding was renewed during recent restoration of the tower, which was carried out with financial support from English Heritage.

The great herbaceous borders flanking the lawns were designed by Graham Stuart Thomas in the 1960s, with a scheme of soft colours on one side and strong colours on the other. There are also magnificent mulberry trees and groups of young False Acacias.

THE EXTERIOR OF THE HOUSE (7)

The inscription that runs round all four sides of the entablature was provided by W. E. Gladstone and offers a useful summary of the complex architectural history of Cliveden:

North Front: AEDIFICATA FUNDAMENTIS A GEO VILLIERS BUCKINGHAMIAE DUCE OLIM LOCATIS REGE CAROLO SECONDO (Built on the foundations laid by George Villiers, Duke of Buckingham in the reign of Charles II)

South Front: INSTAURATA DOMUM II PRIUS IBIDEM IGNE ABSUMPTIS A GEO DUCE SUTHERLANDIAE ET HENRIETTA UXORE (Established by George, Duke of Sutherland and his wife Henrietta after the second house formerly on the same site had been destroyed by fire)

East Front: EXSTRUCTA A.D. MDCCCLI ANNUM IAM XIV DEO AUSP REGNANTE VICTORIA (Constructed in the year 1851, the fourteenth year of Victoria's glorious reign)

West Front: POSTIA INGENIO OPERA CONSILIO CAROLI BARRY ARCHIT. A MDCCCLI (The work accomplished by the brilliant plan of the architect Charles Barry in 1851)

The only feature of the exterior not originally designed by Charles Barry in 1850–1 is Clutton's *porte-cochère* of 1869–70. However, the disposition of the north front still follows almost exactly the plan of William Winde's house built for the Duke of Buckingham in the 1670s, and Thomas Archer's wings and curving colonnades added on either side for Lord Orkney 30 years later. Yet practically none of the original structure remains. The colonnades survived the fire of 1795 only to perish in that of 1849, while the east (guest) wing (on the left-hand side facing the house) was rebuilt in 1886 by the Duke of Westminster and only returned to its present form, matching the west (servants') wing after the 1st Lord Astor moved to Cliveden in 1893. In fact all that exists of the two earlier houses on the site is part of the internal structure of the west wing – its exterior having been rendered in cement and its pediment removed by Barry to complement his main block, in 1851. A tunnel under the middle of the courtyard for the use of servants, connecting the two wings, also survives.

The house was thoroughly repaired in 1984–5. Cracked or perished patches of render were replaced with 'indents', but much of what is seen today is Barry's. A large number of the terracotta balusters had lost their protective skin and had to be replaced. This was the first and major element in a repair programme that has now advanced to the other main structures including the clock-tower, terrace and balustrades. Box hedges were planted around the house in the late 1980s to provide a dark green 'plinth' between the gravel drive and the façade. The interior is used by Cliveden Hotel Ltd, though three principal rooms (see Chapter Eight) are regularly open to the public.

THE DUKE'S GARDEN AND UPPER TERRACE (9)

The garden reached by passing behind the east wing towards the south front of the house takes its name from a pattern of flints on the lawn, last relaid in the late 1980s in the shape of a rapier with the date 1668; it is best seen from the terrace. This commemorates the notorious duel between the Duke of Buckingham and the Earl of Shrewsbury, though this took

The view south from the Upper Terrace over the Parterre

place not at Cliveden but at Barn Elms, near Putney (see p.8). The Duke's Garden had been replanted with borders of evergreen and flowering shrubs, mainly in pink and purple.

The breathtaking view from the upper terrace on the south front – perhaps unequalled at any other English country house – comes as a surprise to visitors approaching from the level plateau north of the entrance side. Beyond the five-acre parterre, the Thames runs in a wide loop with the woods dropping precipitously down towards it. From the time of John Evelyn, who visited in 1679 and found 'a circular view to the uttemost verge of the Horison, which with the serpenting of the *Thames* is admirably surprising', its admirers have included Giuseppe Garibaldi and Queen Victoria. Sir George Warrender would stand here with guests and, with a wave of his arm, pronounce, 'All you can see is mine'. In fact, although the view is framed by the great beechwoods established by Lord Orkney, which stretch from Taplow to Cookham, the Cliveden demesne has always been long and narrow, and most of the extensive landscape has never belonged.

From the time of the Sutherlands until comparatively recently a tent with open sides was usually pitched during the summer in the centre of the terrace, outside the Drawing Room windows, for regular guests to sit in the shade, enjoy the view, sketch, or – in the case of George Bernard Shaw – type. Barry's design also provided for sun-blinds, ingeniously concealed within the upper part of the window frames.

Set into the wall of the house above the windows of Barry's one-storey additions at each end are Caen stone reliefs of *The Four Seasons* by Alexander Munro, which are not shown on Barry's elevation but were noticed here by Sheahan in 1862.

Beyond the façade to the west, the terrace broadens out again into a lawn with statuary collected and arranged by the 1st Lord Astor. The Terrace Pavilion (10), on the west side of the house, was designed as an open loggia with a pantiled roof decorated with anthemions above the gutters in a Greek Revival style by Frederick Pepys Cockerell in the early 1860s.

THE LOWER TERRACE AND BORGHESE BALUSTRADE (11)

Descending by the double staircase in the centre of the south front, the extent of William Winde's immense arcaded 'platforme' becomes apparent for the first time. Eleven blank arches stretch out either side of the stairs with three more open arches in the slightly projecting, rusticated pavilions at each end, making a grand total of 28. The terrace is about 400 feet wide. The projecting ends appear to have been built after the rest of the arcade. The present blind arches of the rest of the terrace appear as niches in eighteenth-century views and it is not clear when they were filled. Barry's great drawing of 1851 also proposed niches.

Behind the large arch in the centre, under the staircase, is the vaulted 'Sounding Room' (so called because of its echo) from whence an internal

staircase, described by Defoe, still rises into the basement of the house. At the time of his visit (1724) this may have been the only stair in the centre of the terrace. Concerts are said to have been given here in Frederick, Prince of Wales's time, though the resonance would surely have defeated all but the slowest *andante*. Today the Sounding Room contains a marble *Venus de' Medici* (23) and a chimney-piece removed from the Astor Estate Office in London. Above the central arch is a marble rounder carved (perhaps by Alexander Munro) with a portrait bust of the Duchess of Sutherland. It was found in a lumber room in the house by the 1st Lord Astor around 1900 and set up here so that, as he put it, the Duchess could for ever look out '... upon the parterre which was her creation forty years ago'.

The gold-painted iron gates to the Sounding Room and the three-bay projecting ends of the terrace were also set up by Lord Astor, and bear his monogram and the date 1895. The end projections were used as aviaries by Frederick, Prince of Wales. By the mid-nineteenth century they had tall sash windows and served as orangeries, the potted trees being carried out to line the lower terrace walk in the summer. They are now known, after their most recent use, as the ferneries. Along the terrace walk today is a series of well-heads collected by the 1st Lord Astor.

Barry's drawing for the south front shows figurative frescos on a dark ground on the walls of the staircase, but these were evidently never executed. From the 1870s these and the walls of the lower terrace have been covered with plants. Today, *Magnolia grandiflora* is grown on the stairs, while the climbers below include *Actinidia chinensis*, *Wistaria sinensis*, *Rosa banksiae* – both double white and double yellow – and *Celastrus orbiculatus*. There are also less vigorous shrubs: an old pomegranate, the sweet-smelling Winter Sweet, and *Viburnum* 'Fulbrook', a superior hybrid of *V. carlesii*.

Running parallel with Winde's terrace, on a bank just above the parterre itself, is the famous balustrade brought from the gardens of the Villa Borghese in Rome, and set up here in 1896 (17). The balustrade and pedestals are of travertine marble, with brick-tile panels behind the seats. It was carved in 1618–19 by the sculptors Giuseppe di Giacomo

The Parterre

and Paolo Massini for one of the greatest art collectors and patrons of Baroque Rome, Cardinal Scipione Borghese. The pedestals at each end are carved with the dragons and eagles of the house of Borghese, and those at the centre have small fountain basins into which grotesque masks spew a constant stream of water. Lord Astor was unable to purchase the antique statues that stood on the main pedestals in Rome (see p.41) and later substituted two eighteenth-century French marble statues (*27, 28*) commissioned for Louis XIV's garden at Marly.

THE PARTERRE (12, 13)

The form of the great plateau beyond the balustrade has changed little since Lord Orkney began his garden in 1706 (see p.48), though the pattern and content of the planting certainly has. Today's scheme of interlocking beds filled with *Santolina incana*, *Senecio* 'Sunshine' and *Nepeta* 'Six Hills

Giant' edged with box is derived from the layout imposed by John Fleming, head gardener to the Duchess of Sutherland from the 1850s. Fleming's beds were edged with chipped privet and spruce, and filled with azaleas and rhododendrons. Spaces were left for hollyhocks, gladioli and foxgloves, and summer and spring bedding. In between the triangular beds, Fleming placed round ones filled with roses. The present sentinel yews were planted by the National Trust in 1976. Fleming also planted the plain, raised ring of grass at the southern end of the lawn with flowering shrubs. About 1906 Waldorf Astor set up the bronze of *The Rape of Proserpina* (*16*), which his father had bought at the same time as the Borghese Balustrade. It is attributed to the Florentine Vincenzo de' Rossi, and dates from around 1565. The piece now on display is a copy; the original is on long-term loan to the Victoria and Albert Museum.

THE TORTOISE FOUNTAIN (14)

Immediately to the west of the ring, steps lead down between the trees to a promontory, giving views across the river to the pastures, hedgerows and lines of Lombardy poplars (many of them planted by the 2nd Viscount Astor to mark the boundary of his land and to screen out the glimpses of suburbia beyond) in the valley. Designs for the stone fountain ornamented with tortoises (*34*), and for the surrounding balustrades (smaller versions of the Borghese Balustrade) were provided by the sculptor Waldo Story in the 1890s.

THE OCTAGON TEMPLE (15)
AND YEW TREE WALK (16)

About half-way down the west side of the Parterre, on the edge of the chalk cliffs above the river can be seen the green copper dome of the Octagon Temple, designed by Giacomo Leoni in the last years of Lord Orkney's life. The building contract still exists, signed by Leoni and the mason Edward Vickers, together with a letter dated June 1735 in which he refers to the joiner, named Power, beginning on 'ye framing of ye Cupollo'. The design went through several stages; four different versions survive in Leoni's hand, and there is a fifth by James Gibbs – the only known appearance at Cliveden of this famous architect.

As originally built, the temple had a pedimented doorcase on the east side facing the Parterre, which led into a 'Prospect-room', of which Jeremiah Milles in 1743 recorded, 'Ye ceiling is prettily done in fretwork and ye Architecture is not amiss.' Under this, approached from the lower terrace walk on the west side, was 'a little cool room, by way of grotto', described in the 1818 sale particulars as a 'tea room with an ornamented dome ceiling'. The rusticated red-brick basement may have been rendered.

This building was quite transformed after the purchase of Cliveden by the 1st Viscount Astor in 1893. With the architect Frank Pearson he converted it into a family chapel, with the interior reduced to a single cruciform space and the dome and upper walls ornamented in colourful mosaic to designs by Clayton & Bell. In the lower parts the subjects are arranged as New Testament 'types' and Old Testament 'antitypes' – eg *The Serpent Tempting Eve* versus *The Annunciation*. In the principal tier are scenes from the life of Christ, above a series of seated saints. In the dome are Our Lord and the Blessed Virgin Enthroned, and the archangels. The stained-glass windows (six figures of Virtues) are also by Clayton & Bell, and the altar furniture by Barkentin & Krall. Lord Astor, his son and daughter-in-law, their son the 3rd Viscount, and Robert Gould Shaw, Nancy Astor's son by her first marriage, are all buried here.

With the conversion to a single storey, the door to the upper level on the east side was blocked and a memorial plaque set up later in its place, recording the names of staff at Cliveden and White Place Farm who fell in the First World War. The two large carved stone urns on pedestals which flank the temple on this side were carved by Thomas Greenaway of Bath in 1725.

The altar in the Octagon Temple

Canning's Oak

The Yew Tree Walk, descending by 172 steps, leads southwards from the temple, descending sharply, though almost in a straight line, nearly parallel with the river. The yews were probably planted by Lord Orkney and kept neatly trimmed, but they were allowed to grow more freely from the end of the eighteenth century. By 1904 they were all but completely overhanging the path, and have since been cut down to re-grow. The eastern row of yews was planted in 1985.

THE WAR MEMORIAL GARDEN (17) AND CANNING'S OAK (18)

Following the lower path from the Octagon Temple northwards, an opening on the right leads into a sunken secret garden, cut out of the steep slope and shaded by trees. This was excavated and lined with tufa rocks by the 1st Viscount Astor in 1902 and originally conceived as an Italian garden, with fragments of Roman sculpture (*10*) arranged here as other parts of his collection were, a few years later, at Hever. In 1917–18, however, the garden was adapted as a cemetery for those who had died in the Canadian Red Cross Hospital on the Cliveden estate from wounds inflicted in the Great War. The 1st Lord Astor's mosaic floor was replaced by turf, in which were set 42 inscribed stones marking the graves. At the centre of one side is a bronze female figure by Sir Bertram MacKennal, RA (35), intended to represent Canada. For the head the sculptor used the features of Lady Astor, though she insisted it was not to be a recognisable portrait.

Continuing northwards, the almost parallel straight paths along the edge of the steep hill are remains of the layout created for Lord Orkney in the early 1720s by Charles Bridgeman, and many of the large yews are again relics of hedges or topiary from that period. When John Loveday visited Cliveden in 1734 he described 'the Trees in the Garden ... forced to be upheld by Ropes, otherwise the Winds would tear 'em down'. One tree along this path is of particular importance, an oak of great age (older even than the first Cliveden House), which has come to be known as Canning's Oak. Tradition has it that the great statesman George Canning (1770–1827), who was a frequent guest of Lord and Lady Inchiquin at Taplow Court in the early 1800s, used to spend hours seated beneath its branches, enjoying the superb view down the river.

THE AMPHITHEATRE (19)

Farther to the north, just as the clearing in front of the Blenheim Pavilion opens out, a steep straight path on the left leads to the Amphitheatre.* Another survival from Bridgeman's layout of the 1720s for Lord Orkney, this open-air theatre with three semicircular grass tiers is close in form to those made by Bridgeman and William Kent at Claremont in Surrey and Rousham in Oxfordshire, both similarly cut out of steep hillsides. It must have been close to Pope's 'little Bridgemannick theatre' at his villa at Twickenham, turfed in 1726 (significantly, since Pope advised his friend Lord Orkney on the

---

* This feature is more properly a (single) *theatre* than a (double) *amphitheatre*, but since the misnomer was first applied by Lord Orkney himself, it has stuck.

Cliveden garden in the 1730s; it may even have been Pope who introduced Bridgeman here).

The theatre was regularly used when Cliveden was occupied by Frederick, Prince of Wales. Artificial scenery was rarely employed, and lighting was set up in the surrounding trees. It was here in August 1740 that Thomas Arne's music for the *Masque of Alfred*, with the concluding ode, 'Rule, Britannia!', was first performed.

THE BLENHEIM PAVILION (20) AND QUEEN ANNE'S VASE (21)

Returning to the clearing above the Amphitheatre, a path leads round to the Blenheim Pavilion on the northern boundary of the garden. Like the Octagon Temple, this was designed for Lord Orkney by Giacomo Leoni. Its date is uncertain, but it may be around 1727, the date of Leoni's designs for rebuilding Cliveden House (see p.15). As well as a great national victory, Blenheim was Lord Orkney's own finest hour as a general, and he most probably christened the pavilion, with its martial pediment, himself. Leoni's drawing showed a 'bagno' and water closet at the back of the building but if these amenities were ever installed, they have since disappeared. More recently, a life-size bronze of the

The Blenheim Pavilion

The Long Garden

great Duke of Marlborough, commissioned from Waldo Story by Lord Astor and placed in the centre of the pavilion, was destroyed by vandals, who also severely damaged the building.

On the east side of the clearing in front of the Blenheim Pavilion is a large early eighteenth-century urn on a pedestal, seen to its most dramatic effect from the Shell Fountain at the far end of the straight vista to the east. Known as Queen Anne's Vase and reputed to have been given by her to Lord Orkney, it is probably slightly later in date, with its

Kentian ornament of carved lion masks and drapery and its Greek key pattern. The inscription on the pedestal is a late nineteenth-century addition.

THE LONG GARDEN (22)

Immediately to the east of the Blenheim Pavilion, just inside the high brick boundary wall on the Hedsor road, is the Long Garden, created by the 1st Viscount Astor. His inspiration was clearly the Renaissance and seventeenth-century gardens he had known during his years as US Minister in Italy, with their statuary and formal evergreens. A wide mown walk down the centre, bordered with box hedges and topiary, leads to a central space with four eighteenth-century stone figures from the *Commedia dell' Arte* – Beatrice, Brighella, Arlecchino and Colombina (*18*). Two more eighteenth-century figures (*19*, *20*) at the far end of the garden are Venetian; the female figure is an allegory of navigation, and the male an unidentified historical figure, traditionally called 'Marco Polo'.

The central beds were originally filled with herbaceous plants under the guidance of Norah Lindsay. Today they are permanently planted with *Euonymus fortunei* 'Variegatus' relieved by 'dot plants' of *Yucca gloriosa*. On the long south-facing wall are several unusual shrubs, the narrow-leaved and the Californian Sweet Bays, *Buddleia auriculata*, so fragrant in autumn, *Actinidia kolomikta*, with pink foliage, *Calycanthus fertilis* or Nutmeg bush, *Dipelta floribunda*, *Ribes speciosum* (a Californian gooseberry with scarlet, fuchsia-like flowers), *Drimys winteri*, *Azara microphylla* from South America, and *Staphylea colchica*.

THE ILEX GROVE (23)

To the south of the Long Garden, on the western side of the main drive, is a plantation consisting largely of evergreen oak, *Quercus ilex*, which were probably planted to a Bridgeman design for Lord Orkney. The sinuous depressions in the lawns today mark the lines of the famous 'ribbon borders' with which John Fleming entwined the Grove in the 1860s. At the same time the Duke and Duchess of Sutherland placed a number of statues here. On a rocky cairn towards the northern end was placed the copy of William's Theed's *Prince Albert in Highland Dress* (*30*), presented by the widowed Queen Victoria to her widowed friend, the Duchess, in 1865. The cairn is surrounded with heather, and by the rose 'Félicité et Perpetué', first raised by the Duc d'Orléans' gardener in 1827.

Amongst the other statuary in the Grove is a large Neo-classical urn carved in granite and commemorating the 1st Earl of Ellesmere, younger brother of the 2nd Duke of Sutherland, and the bronze statue of *Joan of Arc* (*29*) by Princesse Marie d'Orléans, a frequent visitor to Cliveden in her day.

THE SECRET GARDEN (24)

This hidden feature, previously known as the Rose Garden, is a fluid design of curved beds with a gravel path set within a lawn, itself set in an earlier circle of yew trees that was set out in 1959 by Sir Geoffrey Jellicoe. In the eighteenth century a bowling green occupied this site, later a tennis court and then a rose garden, laid out by the 3rd Lord Astor, which included the Wounded Amazon. This sculpture was carved by the young William Waldorf (later 1st Viscount Astor), probably in the studio of William Wetmore Story (see p. 59). The Jellicoe layout was refurbished in 1993 with the help of funds from the National Gardens Scheme. Because 'rose sickness' has affected the vigour of the display, a planting scheme using herbaceous perennials and grasses is rejuvenating the design.

THE WATER GARDEN (25)

Beyond the car-park a path leads eastwards to the Water Garden. Until 1893 this area consisted of parkland with a small stagnant duck pond. Soon afterwards Lord Astor enlarged the pond for skating, and created the island by digging a canal around it. The pond, which now contains golden carp and orfe, was further enlarged by the 2nd Lord Astor in 1905. The pagoda on the island, made for the Paris Exposition Universelle of 1867, was bought at the sale of Bagatelle, Lord Hertford's villa in the Bois de Boulogne, in 1900. The island and pagoda were restored in 1980–3.

On the banks of the pond are numerous moisture-loving plants: King Cups in spring, followed by primulas, irises, astilbes, day-lilies and Purple Loosestrife, accompanied by various Japanese azaleas and rhododendrons. The flat surface of the water contrasts with outcrops of rock, a stone bridge, water-lilies and the giant leaves of *Gunnera manicata*. In spring, scillas grow under bush wisteria, and in one approach to the garden white daffodils are spread under Japanese cherries. The plantings have been extended in the last 15 years and a gravel path now gives access in all seasons.

The Water Garden

THE CAPTAIN'S FIELD (26)

What is now the overflow car-park beyond the Water Garden, formerly known as the Captain's Field, is planted with eight species and two hybrids of *Catalpa*, the Indian bean tree, part of the National Collection of the genus, held in association with the National Council for the Conservation of Plants and Gardens.

THE RUSSIAN VALLEY (27) AND SPRING DRIVE (28)

The gently curving valley to the east of the house, through which the main drive now passes, derived its curious name simply from a corruption of the word 'rushy'. Two ponds, which are due to be restored, formerly existed at its head, and a stream still flows (mostly underground) down the valley to the river. Originally scattered woodland, the valley was cleared by the Duke of Westminster soon after he acquired Cliveden in 1869. John Fleming supervised the work, which was completed by 1872, when the editor of *The Garden* praised it as 'undoubtedly one of the finest things that has been done in the way of landscape gardening near London for many years'. The drive continuing down the hill, rather than forking left back to the Feathers Gate, descends to the bank of the Thames and unmistakably into the world of Jerome K. Jerome's *Three Men in a Boat*. The two-mile extent of Cliveden Reach, from Cookham to Boulter's Lock, has been called the most beautiful on the entire river. Along the bank are disposed a group of picturesque brick, half-timbered and tile-hung cottages designed by George Devey for the Duke and Duchess of Sutherland in the 1850s (see p.33) –

Fallen beech with a prospect of Cliveden; by Carl Laubin, 1988 (Foundation for Art)

THE PACKWAY (29)
AND DUKE'S SEAT (30)

A further length of Story's copy of the Borghese Balustrade can be found behind the boathouse, along with a fragment of an ancient road known as the Packway. It leads, by a zigzag path up through the woods, to the so-called Duke's Seat, where the Duke of Sutherland's statue was placed in 1896. On the way, at a point known as the Half Moon, is the 1st Lord Astor's most eccentric addition to the grounds: the widest section (16ft 6in) of a Californian redwood (*Sequoia gigantea*) in the United Kingdom. It was brought here in this form from California in 1897. The bark, about two inches thick, had to be removed in order to fit the section into the hold of the ship. The Duke's statue (*31*) was carved by Matthew Noble in 1866, originally for the end of the Grand Avenue, where it was supplanted by Story's *Fountain of Love* (*32*). The new site was a happy choice, since the Duke's mansion appears nowhere more magnificently than from here, across the beechwoods.

From the Duke's Seat, visitors can take the Grand Walk for a further mile and three-quarters to the south along the top of the bluff, returning the same way or (via a steep path) to the riverside walk which emerges at the boathouse, or cross to the east via the Woodlands car-park to join the Green Drive, an early eighteenth-century ride which extends in a straight line for more than one mile down the eastern edge of the estate. The restoration of the walks and rides was begun in the early 1980s with the proceeds of the Cliveden Hanging Woods Appeal. Since the loss of over 2,000 canopy trees in the Great Storms of 1987 and 1990, the task has become far greater, but further funds have been made available from the National Trust's Storm Disaster Appeal.

Rose Cottage, New Cottage, Ferry Cottage (the former ferry can be seen working in Henry Taunt's photograph), Seven Gables and Spring Cottage, with Devey's boathouse between the last two.

In the 1890s Thomas Waldo Story laid out an elegant bridge with urns, balustrades (based on the Borghese Balustrade), and steps down to the water's edge in the garden of Spring Cottage, a favourite landing place for two centuries because of the mineral spring nearby. A riverside walk with spectacular views back to the house continues to the south behind Spring Cottage (neither the cottage nor its garden are open to the public). Visitors can return the same way or climb to the Grand Walk along the hillside above.

(Left) Rose Cottage, photographed by Henry Taunt in the mid-nineteenth century

CATALOGUE OF GARDEN SCULPTURE

1 ROMAN, AD c.200–250
Oval fluted sarcophagus
Marble
Carved with amphora in the central ellipse, and lions, with their keepers, attacking a foal at the left end and a boar at the right. [North Forecourt]

2 ROMAN, AD c.200–250
Oval fluted sarcophagus
Marble
With a small figure of a draped woman in the central ellipse of the fluting, and at each of the ends a lion, accompanied by his keeper, tearing to pieces the carcase of an ox. [North Forecourt]

3 ROMAN, AD c.230
Sarcophagus with the Triumph of Bacchus
Marble
Bacchus drives his panther-drawn chariot on the left, bringing up the rear of the Bacchic procession, which is headed by Heracles in a lion-skin on the right. The procession includes two Indian captives, one riding on an elephant, the other on a camel.

Formerly in the Morelli collection, Florence. Acquired from the Villa Borghese. Many restorations including a large central section. [North Forecourt]

4 ROMAN, AD c.230
Sarcophagus with Endymion
Marble
Luna, conducted by Hymenaeus, descends from her chariot towards the reclining Endymion, over whom Somnus pours a sleeping potion. Below the horses Tellus, the personification of the Earth, turns towards a seated herdsman. The corner figures represent the four seasons, and above them are the chariot of the sun (top left) and the setting moon (top right). From the Villa Borghese. Extensively restored. [North Forecourt]

5 ROMAN, AD c.100
Sarcophagus with cupids
Marble
Four cupids bearing garlands on their shoulders. In the spaces between these, from left to right, a tragic

(6) Theseus sarcophagus (North Forecourt)

(4) Endymion sarcophagus (North Forecourt)

female mask, a male portrait bust, and a comic slave's mask, with a griffin at each end. From the Villa Taverna, Frascati. This sarcophagus was apparently not made to order but kept 'in stock', with the central portrait left incomplete to be given the features of the deceased. In fact this was left to the nineteenth-century restorer, who also reworked the left-hand griffin. [North Forecourt]

6 ROMAN, AD *c.*240–250
Sarcophagus with Theseus
Marble
Representing scenes from the story of Theseus and Ariadne. To the left of the central pilaster, Theseus meeting the bearded King Minos; at the right-hand corner of the front panel, Theseus stands over the head of the Minotaur, while Daedalus urges him to flee from Crete; immediately to the right of the central pilaster, Theseus sails away from Naxos in a boat, abandoning the reclining Ariadne.

The sarcophagus was found in 1883 at Castel Giubileo, the site of ancient Fidenae north of Rome, with a fragment of the lid inscribed with a dedication to a certain Artemidorus by his mother Valeria. The heads of the three figures of Theseus probably portray Artemidorus, while that of Ariadne is a likeness of Valeria. [North Forecourt]

7 ROMAN, AD *c.*150–200
Oblong fluted sarcophagus
Marble
A group of Cupid and Psyche in the central panel and a Victory carrying a garland at each corner. On the reverse, the profile bust of a Renaissance

nobleman between armorial shields, suggesting that the sarcophagus was turned around and reused, perhaps in the fifteenth century, when the griffins at each end were probably re-worked. [North Forecourt]

8 ROMAN, AD *c.*150–200
Oblong fluted sarcophagus
Marble
In the central panel Bacchus accompanied by Pan and a panther. To the left and right, a satyr with a wine-skin and a maenad playing a flute. [North Forecourt]

9 ROMAN, AD *c.*150–200
Oblong fluted sarcophagus
Marble
Cupid and Psyche in the central panel, with cupids at each end carrying garlands. [West Upper Terrace]

10 ROMAN
Architectural fragment
Arranged by W. W. Astor, including two Corinthian capitals from the second century AD mounted on columns of different origin (one spiral-fluted); two other Corinthian capitals; three broken columns (only one of which is ancient); a 'Palmyrene' leaf-capital, second century AD; a pilaster fragment with decorative relief pattern of wine jugs, first century AD; a relief of the Crucifixion supported on a second-century AD column on a later plinth. [War Memorial Garden]

11 ROMAN, first-century AD
Funerary relief
Marble
Two cupids in high relief hold a garland of fruit. Probably part of a funerary monument. The surrounding marble frame with griffin consoles is of different origin and probably not ancient. [War Memorial Garden]

12 ROMAN, first-century AD
Head of a bearded man
Marble
Mounted as a term. A copy of a fifth-century BC Greek original. [War Memorial Garden]

13 ROMAN
Double-sided head of a boy
Marble
[War Memorial Garden]

14 ROMAN
Head of a woman
Marble
Mounted as a term. A Roman copy of an idealised Greek original. [War Memorial Garden]

15 ROMAN
Head of a young man
Marble
Mounted as a term. Perhaps an African. [War Memorial Garden]

16 Attributed to VINCENZO DE' ROSSI (1525–87)
Rape of Proserpina, *c.*1565
Bronze
Bought by W. W. Astor at the same time as the Borghese Balustrade, this group was made for the Florentine patrician Giovan Vettorio Soderini (1527–97). In 1594 it passed to another Florentine, Antonio Salviati (1554–1619), in whose collection it was preserved until *c.*1892. [Parterre; a copy. The original is on long-term loan to the Victoria and Albert Museum]

17 GIUSEPPE DI GIACOMO and PAOLO MASSINI
Borghese Balustrade, 1618–19
Travertine and brick tile
Bought by W. W. Astor in 1896 from the Villa Borghese in Rome, where it enclosed the south forecourt. Alternating balustrade and seats, its ends are formed as pedestals carved with the Borghese dragon and eagle, with semicircular basins on three sides. [Lower Terrace]

18 NORTH ITALIAN, eighteenth-century
Figures from the *Commedia dell'Arte*: *Beatrice, Brighella, Arlecchino* and *Colombina*
Istrian stone
These figures, originally from a garden in Padua, belong to a North Italian tradition of figurative sculpture for villa gardens on the Venetian mainland. They relate to similar figures carved in the workshops of Antonio Bonazza (1698–1763) and Orazio Marinali (1643–1720). [Long Garden]

19 Attributed to GIUSEPPE TORRETTO (1661–1743)
Nautica
Marble
This figure, symbolising navigation, has marine attributes arranged on the base and the pouting head of *Wind* under her right foot. Stylistically she

(17) One of the travertine fountains that form the ends of the Borghese Balustrade

(19) Nautica, Long Garden

can be compared with other sculptures carved by Torretto for churches in Venice and the Venetian mainland. [Long Garden]

20 VENETIAN, eighteenth-century
'Marco Polo' wearing the costume of a 'Capitano del Mar'
Marble
The traditional identification of this figure as Marco Polo may be incorrect, and his costume suggests that this may be a historicising portrait of a member of the Morosini family. W. W. Astor described the figure as 'Doge Morosini'. Acquired with no.18 from the Gatterburg-Morosini sale in Venice in 1894. [Long Garden]

21 BERTEL THORVALDSEN (1770–1843)
Mercury about to kill Argus, 1818
Marble
The first version was commissioned in 1818 by Duke Christian August of Augustenburg, but purchased by Alexander Baring in 1822. The water mark on a drawing of the Cliveden version in the Sutherland Papers is dated 1846. It was no doubt bought in Rome by the 2nd Duke; the Duke had commissioned a bust from Thorvaldsen while on his Grand Tour in 1818. [Ilex Grove]

22 RINALDO RINALDI (1793–1873)
The Delphic Sibyl
Marble; signed R.RINALDI.F
On a pedestal with an inlaid lead inscription (later and inapposite: 'Joys we shall have/that blossomed in the shade/And grief that out of sweetest dreams/Awoke.'
This figure, by one of Canova's most devoted students, was commissioned by the Duchess of Sutherland. Rinaldi was popular among the British aristocracy and counted among his patrons the Dukes of Devonshire and Westminster. [Walk below the Amphitheatre]. Replaced at Stafford House by Marachetti's *Erin*.

23 ITALIAN, nineteenth-century
Venus de' Medici
Marble
Perhaps acquired by the 2nd Duke of Sutherland on his Grand Tour. [Sounding Room]

24 ITALIAN, nineteenth-century
Diana
Marble
Shown as a huntress. A loose variant of an 18th-century French type. [Ilex Grove]

25 ITALIAN
Venus
Pentelic marble
Perhaps from a fountain. Incomplete, but restored. Loosely based on the *Venus d'Este* type. [Secret Garden]

26 ITALIAN, nineteenth-century
Satyr resting
Marble
Base on the Hadrianic 'Marble Faun' in the Capitoline Museum at Rome, a copy after a Greek original. [Secret Garden]

27 CLAUDE POIRIER (1656–1729)
Handmaiden of Diana, c.1713–18
Marble; signed
[Lower Terrace: currently undergoing conservation]

28 CLAUDE-AUGUSTIN CAYOT (1677–1722)
Handmaiden of Diana, c.1713–18
Marble; signed
These two handmaidens were commissioned by Louis XIV to accompany a classical statue of Diana for the park at Marly, although neither was ever set up there. They were bought by W. W. Astor from Lord Hertford's house at Bagatelle near Paris. [Lower Terrace; currently undergoing conservation]

29 Princesse MARIE-CHRISTINE D'ORLÉANS (1813–39)
Joan of Arc, c.1838
Bronze (cast by Eck et Durand); signed with monogram: 'MO'
Inscribed on the marble pedestal are the words: 'Jeanne D'Arc Par La Princesse Marie D'Orléans' (right); 'Elle Aimait Tant la France' (left)
[Ilex Grove]

30 WILLIAM THEED the Younger (1804–91)
Prince Albert (1819–61) in Highland Dress
Bronze; signed and dated 1865
After a marble at Balmoral (1863), given by the Queen to her Mistress of the Robes, the Duchess of

(30) Prince Albert in Highland Dress; by William Theed the Younger, 1865 (Ilex Grove)

Sutherland (both of them were widowed in 1861). The figure is exceptionally finely modelled, especially in the coat of the setter and the hatching of the stock of the Prince's shotgun. There are four unsigned drawings in the Cliveden Album for the placing of the statue in a niche on the east face of the clock-tower, but since another bronze replica set up at Balmoral in 1867 stands on an identical rocky cairn it seems likely that this was the original treatment. [Ilex Grove]

31 MATTHEW NOBLE (1818–76)
George Granville Leveson-Gower, 2nd Duke of Sutherland (1786–1861), 1866
Marble
A bronze replica is at Dunrobin. Originally placed at the end of the Grand Avenue, it was moved to this position in 1896. [Duke's Seat]

32 WILLIAM WALDORF ASTOR, 1st VISCOUNT ASTOR (1848–1919)
The Wounded Amazon
Marble; signed and dated 1870
This may be the only extant signed sculpture by Lord Astor. He must have learnt the art in the studio of his acquaintance William Wetmore Story, and it is tempting to suppose that this figure was carved under Story's close supervision. Its composition is dependent on Roman and Hellenistic copies of Greek *Amazons*, but reinterpreted in a Romantic, almost sentimental mood. [Rose Garden]

33 THOMAS WALDO STORY (1855–1915)
The Fountain of Love
Siena/Carrara marble and tufa; inscribed 'Waldo Story Roma 1897'
Designed and carved in Rome by the son and pupil of the American dilettante sculptor William Wetmore Story (1819–95). According to 1st Lord Astor's note of 1920, 'The female figures are supposed to have discovered the fountain of love, and to be experiencing the effects of its wonderful elixir.' [Grand Avenue]

34 THOMAS WALDO STORY (1855–1915)
'Tortoise' Fountain
Travertine
The tortoises on the rims of the bowl recall Taddeo Landini's fountain of 1568 in Piazza Mattei in Rome, where Story had his studio. [Parterre]

35 Sir BERTRAM MACKENNAL, RA (1863–1931)
Female figure, 1917
Bronze; inscribed: 'They are at peace/God/proved them and found them/worthy for/himself'
A successful Australian sculptor, MacKennal studied in London, Paris and Rome, and his work displays the influence of French Symbolist and Romantic art. This figure was commissioned for the War Memorial Garden by Nancy Astor and intended as a personification of Canada (whose fallen soldiers are buried in the surrounding garden). On condition that it was not made known at the time, Lady Astor allowed her own features to be used for the head. [War Memorial Garden]

CHAPTER EIGHT
TOUR OF THE HOUSE

Visitors enter the house by the west wing, adjacent to the clock-tower.

The west and east wings, linked at first to the house by curving colonnades, were built by Thomas Archer for Lord Orkney in 1706, to provide further bedrooms when the main block was reduced in height by a storey. Originally of brick, the wings were rendered in cement and their pediments removed by Sir Charles Barry to complement his new main block in 1851. The west wing was then given over to kitchens and domestic offices. It was restored to its original purpose in 1985 when Cliveden Hotel Ltd built new bedrooms.

The staircase with twisted balusters survives from the eighteenth century, but not in its original position.

THE WEST WING CORRIDOR

PICTURES

FERDINAND ROYBET (1840–1920)
The Oyster Eaters

ENGLISH SCHOOL
Edward VII in Academic Robes

AMERICAN, 1865
Margaret Rebecca Astor (1800–72)
Wife of the above.

GEORGE AUGUSTUS BAKER (1821–80)
William Backhouse Astor (1792–1875), 1870
Grandfather of William Waldorf, 1st Viscount Astor.

Sir ALFRED MUNNINGS, PRA (1878–1959)
A Summer Evening at Cliveden
Waldorf, 2nd Viscount Astor, seated on a shooting stick, with mares and foals at the Cliveden Stud, which he established on the Taplow road (see p.44).

LEONARD RICHMOND (active *c*.1912–40)
The Memorial Garden, Cliveden

FURNITURE

The set of high-backed Italian chairs was reupholstered by members of the Kensington and Chelsea Association of National Trust members in 1985.

THE CURVED CORRIDOR

Archer's colonnades survived the fire of 1795 only to be destroyed in that of 1849; they were rebuilt by Barry for the 2nd Duke of Sutherland. Reminders of the Duke's ownership survive in the form of his cipher (S reversed and interlaced, surmounted by a ducal coronet) present on the panels hung on the walls at either end of the corridor, on the radiator grilles and on the backs of the set of tapestry-covered chairs.

TEXTILES

The standard is embroidered with coloured silks on a black ground with the 'greater' arms of a king of Spain, possibly Philip V (1700–46).

FURNITURE

The carved walnut *buffet* is French, late sixteenth-century, with a representation of the young Louis XIII on a seal on the door of the central cupboard. The large oak *armoire* is a nineteenth-century creation, in the Dutch or Flemish style of 300 years earlier. The early eighteenth-century longcase clock has a japanned case and a month-going movement by Joshua Alsop of London. Hanging in a case near the clock is a stick, designed – according to its inscribed label – 'to push Harriet Duchess of Sutherland uphill from the River to the house'.

PICTURES

RAIMUNDO MADRAZO Y GARRETA (1841–1920)
John Jacob Astor III (1822–90), 1881
Husband of the above.

THOMAS SULLY (1783–1872)
Charlotte Augusta Astor (1825–87), 1860
Mother of William Waldorf, 1st Viscount Astor.

After ELIZABETH VIGÉE BRUN (1755–1842)
Princesse Elisabeth (d.1794)
Oval
The younger sister of Louis XVI, she was executed
in the last weeks of the Terror.

WILLIAM TOMKINS (1730–92)
Cliveden
Shows the house as extended by Thomas Archer for
the Earl of Orkney *c.*1706 and before it was
destroyed by fire in 1795.

SCULPTURE

SIEGFRIED CHAROUX (1896–1967)
Nancy, Viscountess Astor (1879–1964)
Green patinated bronze

T. WHALEN
The flight into Egypt, 1934
Fruitwood

TAPESTRIES

ON LEFT:

*Tomyris ordering the head of Cyrus the Great to be put
in a vessel filled with blood*
Tomyris was queen of a nomadic Central Asian
people. Her army, led by her son, had been tricked
by Cyrus into partaking of a feast. By this tactic
Cyrus was able to slaughter large numbers of his
enemies, and when the young man came to his
senses he killed himself in shame. Tomyris swore to
avenge his death, and in the ensuing battle Cyrus
was killed. Not satisfied, the queen abused the
corpse by ordering the head to be cut off and dipped
in human blood. Another legendary decapitation,
that of Holofernes by Judith, is depicted on the
vessel in which the head is dipped.

ON RIGHT:

Cadmus slaying the dragon
Cadmus, legendary King of Thebes, is on a journey

in search of his sister Europa, who has been carried
off by Zeus disguised as a bull. In the course of the
journey most of his men are killed as they draw
water by the serpent (often depicted as a dragon)
that guards the Spring of Ares. Cadmus slays the
serpent, and is later reconciled to Ares and married
to Harmonia, daughter of Ares and Aphrodite.

Both Brussels, late sixteenth-/early seventeenth-
century.

THE HALL

Practically nothing survives of Barry's original
interior of 1851, and the appearance of these rooms
today is due largely to the 1st Viscount Astor, who
began to remodel them in 1893, soon after he
bought the house, with Frank Pearson as architect.

As designed by Barry the Hall was a far
smaller, square room with a tiled floor resembling
a mosaic, supplied by Minton, and provided a
setting for some of the Sutherlands' contemporary
sculpture, notably the *Joan of Arc* by the Princesse
d'Orléans (*29*). Pearson greatly enlarged the Hall
by opening it through to what was the Morning
Room to the east, and added the oak panelling
and Corinthian columns and pilasters. Nancy Astor
later replaced the Minton-tiled floor with the
present stone flags.

TAPESTRIES

The Art of War: [left to right] *Embuscade, Attaque,
Campement*
Three scenes from the campaigns of the Duke of
Marlborough in the War of the Spanish Succession,
woven at Brussels by Le Clerc and Van der Borch
(by whom they are signed) from cartoons by
Lambert de Hondt, *c.*1710, with borders of martial
trophies centred on the splendid arms which Lord
Orkney 'usurped and assumed for himself' with the
motto of the Order of the Thistle. Marlborough's
conceit of ordering tapestries to commemorate his
own victories from the weavers of the city he had
occupied, to designs originally prepared in 1696 for
his enemy, the Elector Maximilian of Bavaria,
originated with the Blenheim Palace *Art of War* set
in 1706. Subsequently, six of his generals received
their own sets (see note 3 on p.21). There were eight
scenes in de Hondt's cycle, but it is not known

The Hall

whether Lord Orkney had more than the four tapestries that survive (the fourth from the set, *La Marche*, is at Brown University, Providence, Rhode Island).

After his visit to Cliveden in 1734 John Loveday declared that he had seen:

... no Tapestry that excells Lord Orkney's; 'twas made at Brussels on purpose for him; the Colours are extremely lively, yet that is the least commendation of the Arras. 'Tis the siege of Lisle, of the Battle in the Woods [ie Malplaquet] &c. In the latter, the old Miller that was so good a friend to the English, is sitting smoking his pipe ... [see note 10, p.10].

At some time between 1792, when they were seen by another visitor, Archibald Robertson, and 1849, when the Sutherlands purchased Cliveden, they left the house; they were assumed to have been destroyed in one of the fires until they were bought in Paris in the 1890s by the 1st Lord Astor, apparently before their connection with Cliveden was recognised.

FIREPLACE

The stone chimney-piece at the far end of the Hall was bought by Lord Astor at the famous sale of the Spitzer collection in Paris in 1892. It dates from around 1525 and is thought to have come from the château of Arnay-le-Duc in Burgundy. The central niche contains a group of St George and the Dragon.

ITALIAN
Firedogs
Bronze
This pair of bronze figures is typical of the work of the Paduan sculptor Tiziano Aspetti (1565–1607), and stylistically relates to his *atalante* figures for the

chimney-piece of the Sala dell' Anticollegio in the Ducal Palace in Venice. However, this pair was probably cast in the nineteenth century after original bronze figures by Aspetti, of which there are several examples in Italian and US collections.

SCULPTURE

? FERDINANDO TACCA (1619–86)
Ferdinand II de' Medici, Grand Duke of Tuscany (1610–70)
Marble
Inscribed: 'Ferdinando II Medicii DUX Toscane, Tacca fecit 1659'
Although inscribed on the back as by the Florentine sculptor Ferdinando Tacca, the style of the drapery carving suggests that the bust has been reworked at some later date, which might account for the discrepancies over the identification and authorship of this work.

JO DAVIDSON (1883–1952)
Nancy, Viscountess Astor (1879–1964)
Bronze; inscribed 'P.B. 1930'
An American sculptor, Davidson studied in New York and in Paris, where he spent most of his life. He was renowned for his portraits of politicians and generals of the First World War, later portraying prominent literary and political figures of the day.

PICTURES

LEFT OF CHIMNEY-PIECE:

JOHN SINGER SARGENT, RA (1856–1925)
Nancy Langhorne, Mrs Waldorf Astor, later Viscountess Astor, MP (1879–1964)
Signed
Châtelaine of Cliveden from 1906 and the first female MP to take her seat, in 1919. Sargent began the painting in the autumn of 1908. His first intention was to show her carrying her year-old son William Waldorf III piggyback but he eventually decided to paint her alone. The background gave particular trouble and was not resolved until March 1909, when he made her 'bump into a column'. Exhibited RA, 1909. This was one of the last of Sargent's society portraits, as he explained to Nancy Astor in 1910: 'Cliveden is not for me. Together with paughtrut painting I have renounced the polished circles into which it led me for a brief and anxious time.

After Sir PETER LELY (1618–80)
George Villiers, 2nd Duke of Buckingham (1628–87)
Politician, dramatist and libertine, he built the first Cliveden House c.1666 (see Chapter One). The original, painted c.1675, is in the National Portrait Gallery.

After Sir PETER LELY (1618–80)
Anna Brudenell, Countess of Shrewsbury (1642–1702)
A famous beauty, who became the mistress of the 2nd Duke of Buckingham c.1666 and for whom he probably built the first Cliveden House. The original, painted c.1670, is in the National Portrait Gallery.

ENGLISH
George Hamilton, 1st Earl of Orkney (1666–1737)
The Duke of Marlborough's second-in-command

'Campement', from the 'Art of War' series of Brussels tapestries in the Hall

during the War of the Spanish Succession, he purchased Cliveden in 1696 and commissioned Thomas Archer to rebuild the house.

Attributed to HYACINTHE RIGAUD (1659–1743)
Duc de Maine
The eldest son of Louis XIV and his mistress Madame de Montespan.

LEFT OF DOOR TO FRENCH DINING ROOM:

PHILIPPE MERCIER (?1689–1760)
Frederick, Prince of Wales (1707–51) with Princesses Anne (1709–59), Caroline (1713–57) and Amelia (1711–86) Making Music at Kew
Frederick, the first of the Hanoverians to show any interest in the visual arts, appointed Mercier his Principal Portrait Painter in 1729. In 1733, the probable date of this picture, he took up the bass-viol and then the cello with enthusiasm and is shown here being accompanied on the harpsichord and mandora by two of his sisters, while a third sits with a volume of Milton in her lap. The harmony, however, is misleading, as Frederick and the Princess Royal (she is possibly the one shown reading) had very different musical tastes. Mercier painted the prime version, dated 1733 (National Portrait Gallery), and another with a different background (Royal Collection).

The backdrop is the Dutch House at Kew House, which the Princesses inhabited. Between 1731 and 1735 Frederick had William Kent rebuild Kew House as the White House (now gone) opposite the red-brick Dutch House and it is in the grounds of the former that the trio is playing. Frederick later leased Cliveden, from 1737 until his death (see Chapter Two).

An important example of the informal conversation-piece, which Mercier introduced to Britain from France.

ARMOUR

LEFT TO RIGHT:

Three-quarter suit made up as a garniture based on an Italian armour of *c.*1570; Italian helmet with a late sixteenth-century visor; early seventeenth-century arms.

Tilting armour, German or Italian, *c.*1560.

Suit of armour, German, *c.*1560; the legs replaced in the nineteenth century.

Suit of armour with engraved decoration, Italian, late sixteenth-century.

FURNITURE

Much of the furniture is Italian, reflecting the 1st Lord Astor's long residence in Rome and Sorrento, including the large, early seventeenth-century carved walnut table beneath the tapestries, the tall Venetian armchair, the carved and inlaid eighteenth-century walnut chairs in the style of Corradini (bought at the Gatterburg-Morosini sale in 1894) and the seventeenth-century octagonal table on three carved *monopodiae* (single-footed animals).

THE STAIRCASE

The staircase, again designed by Pearson for Lord Astor, has pairs of newel figures carved by W. S. Frith (who later worked extensively for Astor under Pearson's direction at Hever). They represent characters associated with the history of Cliveden (from the bottom):

The 2nd Duke of Buckingham with his mistress, the Countess of Shrewsbury

The 1st Earl and Countess of Orkney

William and Isabella de Turville

William and Alice de Cliveden

Prior John Ramsey

Dorothy Fitzwilliam

Geoffrey de Cliveden

Jack Shepherd

CEILING

The ceiling is one of the only surviving features of the Sutherlands' interior. The figures, painted by the French artist Auguste Hervieu, represent four of their children as the Four Seasons: Spring is Lady Constance Leveson-Gower (afterwards Duchess of Westminster); Summer, Lady Elizabeth (afterwards Duchess of Argyll); Autumn, Lady Caroline (afterwards Duchess of Leinster); and Winter, their eldest son, the Marquess of Stafford. Hervieu taught drawing to the children of Fanny Trollope in the United States and illustrated many of her books.

The ornamental surround was added by J. D. Crace (see p.41).

PICTURES

Studio of THOMAS HUDSON (1701–79)
George II (1683–1760)
The original (now in the National Portrait Gallery) was commissioned in 1744 by Lord Chief Justice Willes, and was, according to Vertue, 'thought very like & a good picture. altho His Majesty did not honour him to set [sit] purposely for it.'

THOMAS HUDSON (1701–79)
Frederick, Prince of Wales (1707–51)
The eldest son of George II (above), whom he loathed, and father of George III. This and its pendant (below) were Hudson's most important royal portraits and provide the best image of the couple in the Prince's last years, but they were not commissioned by Frederick, who preferred the Rococo delicacy of Mercier and Van Loo to Hudson's English sobriety. According to John Faber's engravings of 1751, they were painted from the life in 1750.

THOMAS HUDSON (1701–79)
Augusta, Princess of Wales (1719–72)
The daughter of Frederick II, Duke of Saxe-Gotha, she married the Prince of Wales (above) in 1736, when Lord Hervey thought she was 'rather tall, and had health and youth enough in her face, joined to a very modest and good-natured look, to make her countenance not disagreeable; but her person, from being very ill-made, a good deal awry, her arms long, and her motions awkward, had, in spite of all the finery of jewels and brocade, an ordinary air, which no trappings could cover or exalt.'

After JEAN-BAPTISTE VAN LOO (1684–1745)
Frederick, Prince of Wales (1707–51)
Based on the full-length portrait in robes of state (Royal Collection), painted in 1742, the year Van Loo left England after a very successful five-year stay.

After JEAN-BAPTISTE VAN LOO (1684–1745)
Augusta, Princess of Wales (1719–72)
Pendant to the above.

After FRANZ XAVER WINTERHALTER (1805–73)
Harriet, Duchess of Sutherland (1806–68)
The daughter of 6th Earl of Carlisle, she married the future 2nd Duke of Sutherland (above) in 1823, and was Mistress of the Robes to, and one of the closest friends of, Queen Victoria. The Queen encouraged Winterhalter to paint the original picture (Dunrobin Castle) in 1849, the year the Sutherlands bought Cliveden, and approved the result: 'The Dss is in a court dress with her train over her arm, & quite "dans le grand style".' The Duchess is standing in the staircase hall of the Sutherlands' palatial London home, Stafford (now Lancaster) House, which was designed by Charles Barry in Louis XV style with murals after Veronese. The Cliveden version resembles the oval copy made by William Corden (1819–1900) for the Queen in 1849 (Royal Collection), and may also be by him.

THE FRENCH DINING ROOM

The Rococo *boiseries* with which the room is panelled came, with the marble chimney-piece and painted overdoors, from the Château d'Asnières, not far from Paris, and were acquired by the 1st Lord Astor from the firm of Allard in 1897. The measurements of Barry's dining-room and the room in the Château d'Asnières were virtually identical.

Equal in quality to the finest Louis XV decoration still surviving in France, the room was designed by the architect and *ornemaniste* Nicolas Pineau (1684–1754), whose sketch for the chimney-piece has recently come to light in the Musée des Arts Décoratifs in Paris. Asnières was built in 1750 by the Marquis Le Voyer d'Argenson, at one time Minister of Foreign Affairs and elder brother of the Comte d'Argenson, author of celebrated *Mémoires*. Pineau's designs for the interior of Asnières are dated in this same year and the decoration of the *grand salon* (from which the Cliveden *boiseries* came) with its carved trophies of game, dogs and guns, shows that the house was used primarily as a hunting lodge. Louis XV is reputed to have leased the chateau after the Marquis's death in 1757 and to have lent it to his mistress, Madame de Pompadour; however, the crossed Ls which appear on the chimney-piece (and elsewhere in the room) were probably added by Allard before Lord Astor's purchase.

The Staircase

The French Dining Room

The plasterwork cove and ceiling are partly the original water-gilded work and partly oil-gilded copies of the originals still at Asnières, whereas most of the furniture and the mirrors were made in 1897 to suit the room. Astor originally commissioned a painted ceiling, but this was subsequently replaced by his daughter-in-law.

SCULPTURE

ON CHIMNEY-PIECE:

FRANÇOIS RUDE (1784–1855)
Marquise de Queylar
Dated 1820
A good example of this Neo-classical sculptor's return to Rococo forms after the collapse of the First Empire.

THE DINING ROOM

As built by Barry, there were two drawing-rooms (or a drawing-room and a breakfast-room) here, lined with mirrors to reflect the marvellous view of the Parterre and the Thames below. The two rooms were thrown into one by Clutton for the Duke of Westminster in the 1870s, and then completely remodelled for the 1st Lord Astor by Allard. The room was made into a library by the 2nd Viscount, who installed late seventeenth-century-style panelling. The main drawing-room of the house until 1966, it was adapted for use by the hotel as their main dining-room in 1985.

(Opposite) Looking south along the private terrace of the Lady Astor Suite

BIBLIOGRAPHY

Almost no unpublished papers of the Duke of Buckingham survive. Lord Orkney's family letters are in the National Library of Scotland, MS 1033. The letter from Pope and his military despatches are in Northumberland Record Office, Craster Papers ZCR9. The Andrews survey is in the Buckinghamshire County Record Office in Aylesbury. The papers relating to the English estates of the Duke of Sutherland's family are at Staffordshire Record Office, principally D 593. The archive of the Grosvenor Estate contains some papers relating to Cliveden. The principal unpublished sources for the work of the 1st and 2nd Viscounts Astor are typed memoranda written in 1920 and 1944 respectively, in the possession of Lord Astor (a copy is at the Trust's office at Hughenden Manor), and papers at Reading University. Almost all of the architectural drawings (other than those by Barry and Burn in the RIBA Drawings Collection) are contained in the Cliveden Album, an album in which the 1st Lord Astor assembled drawings and other manuscript and printed material related to Cliveden, in the possession of the present Lord Astor (and see Jackson-Stops, below).

ASTOR, Michael, *Tribal Feeling*, London, 1963.

BARRY, Rev. Alfred, *The Life and Works of Sir Charles Barry*, 1867.

BLISSET, David G., 'Sir Charles Barry (1795–1860): A Reassessment of his Travels and Early Career', PhD thesis, Oxford Polytechnic, 1983.

BOSTRÖM, Antonia, 'A Rediscovered Florentine Bronze Group of the Rape of Proserpina at Cliveden', *Burlington Magazine*, cxxii, December 1990.

BOSTRÖM, Antonia, 'Sculpture at Cliveden: A Connoisseur's Garden', *Apollo*, August 1991.

CHAPMAN, Hester, *Great Villiers: A Study of George Villiers, Second Duke of Buckingham*, London, 1949.

FISKE, Robert, 'A Cliveden Setting', *Music and Letters*, xlvii, 1966.

FLEMING, John, *Spring and Winter Flower Gardening*, 1870.

GOWER, Lord Ronald, *My Reminiscences*, 2 vols, 1883.

HASLAM, Richard, 'Cliveden, Buckinghamshire', *Country Life*, 10 April 1986.

HARRISON, Rose, *Rose, My Life in Service*, 1975.

HUSSEY, Christopher, 'Cliveden I and II', *Country Life*, 11 and 18 July 1931.

HUXLEY, Gervas, *Victorian Duke: The Life of Hugh Lupus Grosvenor, First Duke of Westminster*, London, 1967.

JACKSON-STOPS, Gervase, 'The Cliveden Album: I and II', *Architectural History*, xix and xx, 1976–7.

JACKSON-STOPS, Gervase, 'Formal Garden Designs for Cliveden', *The National Trust Yearbook*, 1976–77, pp.100–17.

JACKSON-STOPS, Gervase, 'Cliveden I and II', *Country Life*, 24 February and 3 March 1977.

JACKSON-STOPS, Gervase, *An English Arcadia*, London, 1992.

LIPSCOMB, George, *History and Antiquities of the County of Buckinghamshire*, iii, 1847.

RICHARDS, Eric, *The Leviathan of Wealth: The Sutherland Fortune in the Industrial Revolution*, London, 1973.

ROBERT, C., 'A Collection of Roman Sarcophagi at Cliveden', *Journal of Hellenic Studies*, xx, 1990.

RORSCHACH, Kinerly, 'Frederick, Prince of Wales as a Collector and Patron', *The Journal of the Walpole Society*, vol. 55, 1993.

SYKES, Christopher, *Nancy: The Life of Lady Astor*, London, 1972.

TYACK, Geoffrey, *Cliveden and the Astor Household between the Wars*, High Wycombe, 1983.

WEAVER, Lawrence, 'Cliveden', *Country Life*, 7 and 14 December 1912.

INDEX